Daisy & Bobby

John Locke

This book is a work of fiction. Names, characters, places and incidents are either the product of the author's imagination or are used fictitiously. Any resemblance to actual persons, living or dead, or to actual events or locales is entirely coincidental.

This eBook is licensed for your personal enjoyment only. This eBook may not be re-sold or given away to other people. If you are reading this eBook and did not purchase it, or it was not purchased for your use only, then you should return it and purchase your own copy. Thank you for respecting the hard work of the author.

DAISY & BOBBY

Cover Designed by: Claudia Jackson
Copyright © iStockPhoto_157307662
Copyright © Fotolia_7315914_M

Published by John Locke Books, LLC

Visit the author's websites:

http://www.donovancreed.com
http://www.daniripper.com

ISBN 978-1-937656-12-6 (eBook)
ISBN 978-1-937656-13-3 (Paperback)

Medical Warning:

Talk to your doctor before beginning a John Locke novel, as studies have shown them to be habit-forming and highly addictive. Do not read Locke if you suffer from high blood pressure or other heart-related issues, as readers often experience mood swings, increased pulses, elevated heart rates, and have reported unexpected shifts in body position that take them to the edge of their seats. Do not drive or use machinery while reading Locke novels.

Locke novels are not for everyone, and may cause serious reactions including insomnia, night terrors, and uncontrollable, maniacal laughter. Tell your doctor right away if you have these, or if you experience unusual changes in your behavior including increased sexual urges, palpitations, or prolonged erections. Common side effects include confusion, hysteria, and trouble swallowing a given premise.

Do not drink alcohol while reading Locke novels, though those with a history of drug or alcohol abuse may be more prone to understanding the material. Adverse reactions to Locke novels include nausea and vomiting, loss of appetite, severe itching, rectal bleeding, purple spots under the skin, and Jimmy Legs. In extreme cases, readers have reported laughing so hard they not only shit their pants, but other's pants, as well. Upon completing a Locke series be prepared to experience symptoms of withdrawal, including fear, anger, extreme sadness, and moderate to severe depression.

Ask your doctor today if John Locke novels are right for you!

Personal Message from John Locke:

I love writing books! But what I love even more is hearing from readers. If you enjoyed this or any of my other books it would mean the world to me if you'd click the link below so you can be on my notification list. That way you can receive updates, contests, prizes, and savings of up to 67% on eBooks immediately after publication!

Just access this link: http://www.DonovanCreed.com, and I'll personally thank you for trying my books.

Also, if you get a chance, I hope you'll check out Dani's website:

http://www.daniripper.com

John Locke

New York Times Best Selling Author

Guinness World Record Holder for eBook Sales!

Fastest Author in History to sell 1 million eBooks!

8th Member of the Kindle Million Sales Club

(Members include James Patterson, George R.R. Martin, and Lee Child)

*John Locke had 4 of the top 10 eBooks on
Amazon/Kindle at the same time, including #1 and #2!*

...Had 6 of the top 20 books <u>at the same time</u>!

...Had 8 books in the top 43 <u>at the same time</u>!

...Has written 33 books in five years in <u>six separate genres</u>,

<u>All best-sellers</u>!

...Has been published throughout the world in numerous languages

by the world's most prestigious publishing houses!

...Winner, Second Act Magazine's Story of the Year!

...Named by Time Magazine as one of the "Stars of the DIY-Publishing Era"

Wall Street Journal: "John Locke (is) transforming the 'book' business"

Dedication:

To my wonderful readers, with all my love!

Daisy & Bobby

Chapter 1

WHEN DAISY PEPPER met Bobby Cujo, she was standing eight-deep in a line of medical students waiting to stick their fingers in Bobby's asshole.

Moments earlier, he'd been on his back, buck naked on the examination table, with his knees in the air, legs spread apart, as the doctor instructed the twelve men and women to gently probe Bobby's gonads with their thumb and forefinger to feel for abnormalities. Afterward, he rolled over and assumed an ass-up position with his face and upper torso pressed against the table. As one student after the other dug into Bobby's anal cavity attempting to locate his prostate, the guy in front of Daisy sneered, "Can you *believe* this guy? What a *loser!*"

"We all serve in our own way," she replied.

"He probably served time in prison. Probably gets off on it," the guy said. Then he added, "You're hot. Want to meet up afterward?"

"I'll say no, this time."

Now, as the last student removes his latex glove and tosses it in the trash receptacle, Daisy peeks over her shoulder and catches Bobby motioning her to come closer. She ignores him, exits the door with the others, then doubles back and sneaks into the room. When Bobby sees her, he smiles and says: "You know what they call the guy in medical school who finished last in his class?"

"Tell me."

"Doctor."

Though she fails to laugh, he pronounces her heart-stoppingly gorgeous and asks if she'll do him the honor of joining him for lunch.

"You're kidding, right?"

"Not at all. And the best part is I'm available."

"What are the odds?" she deadpans.

"Strange but true. So, what do you say? By the way, I'm Bobby Cujo." He extends his hand.

"Daisy Pepper," she says, staring at his hand without accepting it. "Just to be clear, you're asking me on a *date*? After what just happened in this very *room*?"

Bobby retracts his hand and says, "I realize the odds are slim. But if I didn't at least *ask*, I'd regret it my whole life."

"So," she says. "This is it. This is what it feels like."

"What do you mean?"

"I've finally hit rock bottom."

"Think about it this way, Daisy: all the pressure's off. You've already seen me naked."

"There's that."

"Say yes to the date. It'll be great. You won't be sorry."

"What do you usually tell them?"

"Who?"

"The girls that ask, 'What do you do for a living?' What do you say?"

"I tell them I'm a medical consultant for every major hospital in South Louisiana, and I teach aspiring doctors and nurses how to identify internal illnesses. I tell them my services are in such high demand every hospital within 100 miles has my number on speed dial."

"Does that work?"

He grins. "Like you wouldn't believe!"

"There can't be much money in getting finger-fucked by medical students."

"Eleven bucks an hour."

"You say that with pride."

"Why wouldn't I?"

"You allowed twelve men and women to molest you twice in eight minutes. That's..." She uses her phone to do the math. "A dollar and forty-six cents? Could that be right?"

"Not remotely. See, it doesn't matter if it's only eight minutes. They have to pay me for the whole hour. To put it another way, I'm getting an hour's pay for eight minutes' work."

"Do you *enjoy* it?"

"With *you* I did."

"Well, that's creepy."

He laughs. "I saw you earlier in the parking lot. You're not from around here."

"What gave me away? No mud flaps on my rental car?"

"That, and your voice, and every single thing about you!"

"Is this your way of asking what brought me to South Louisiana?"

He nods.

"I wanted to do something different this year for fall break, something I'd never done before. After considerable thought, I narrowed my options to strolling through the falling leaves in Central Park, and digital sodomy, bayou style."

"And here you are. I'm honored. Was it everything you hoped it'd be?"

"And less."

"This isn't my only job, you know."

"Thank God! What else do you do?"

"I'm a curator."

"You mean like in a museum?"

"More like a shrine. I own a one-of-a-kind religious artifact. People come from all over the world to see it."

"Which artifact is that?"

"I'll tell you at lunch. You get off at noon?"

"Actually, I'm free right now. I'm not a med student. I was just blending in, trying to get away from someone. A guy."

"Is he still here?"

"Nope. Long gone. I could have left an hour ago."

"Why didn't you?"

"Are you kidding? Where else could I get free medical training?" He gives her a look. "You stood in line to finger me?"

"I did."

"Why would you do that if you didn't *have* to?"

"I pride myself on being open to new experiences."

Chapter 2

TWENTY MINUTES LATER, at lunch, Bobby brings it up again: "I can't believe you sexually assaulted me."

"You get *paid* to be sexually assaulted! You're like a hooker, only cheaper."

She removes the toothpick from the top of her hamburger bun and uses it to spear a french fry. Then flicks one end and watches it spin like an airplane propeller. Flicks it a couple more times, pops it in her mouth, swallows. Then says: "Technically, you were gangbanged."

"What do you mean?"

"There were twelve of us."

"The others were doing their job. *You* were molesting me."

She spears another fry, spins it and says, "We *all* molested you, Bobby. The only difference is I didn't pay for the privilege."

"Not to make a big deal out of it, but yeah, they paid a quarter million bucks for med school, and you didn't."

"Are you honestly trying to define sexual assault to a *woman?*"

"Maybe I need to since it's any unwanted sexual advance perpetrated on a person without their consent."

"I see. Oddly, I don't recall you saying no, or asking me to stop. What I *do* recall is me asking if you enjoyed what happened, and you said you did. With *me*."

"Right. Well again, I'm not trying to turn it into a *thing*, I'm just saying there's a double standard: if an unauthorized guy stuck his finger up a woman's ass, she could sue him for everything he has."

"Do I really need to explain why that could never happen?"

"Please do."

"Women don't have prostates."

"Funny. My point is, I help people."

"That's great. Can we move past this now?"

"Of course. Do you find me attractive?"

She arches an eyebrow.

"Reason I ask, you fondled me when you didn't have to, then you came back to the room to meet me, and now we're having lunch."

She pushes the toothpick lengthwise through a french fry, holds it up and rubs it gently with her thumb and forefinger as if simulating masturbation, then puts it in her mouth and slides it in and out as if simulating fellatio. Then she pulls the fry off the toothpick, holds it from the bottom end, and watches it droop, causing Bobby to ask, "Is that supposed to be my dick?"

Daisy says nothing. Just stares at the sad droopy french fry. After a moment, she flicks the tip just hard enough to send several grains of salt flying through the air, symbolizing...well, you get the picture.

Bobby says, "If you're trying to use psychology on me, it won't work."

"Yes," she says.

"Yes, what?"

"I find you attractive. Want to fuck?"

His eyes go huge. "Yes, of course! I mean, do *you* want to?"

"No. I was just trying to gauge your level of interest. I mean, I wouldn't want to spend time with a guy who thinks I'm un-fuckable. Why do you shave your balls?"

"Huh?"

"I couldn't help but notice you were completely shaved. Why?"

"Women like it."

"I don't."

"Why not?"

"It's dangerous."

When he laughs, Daisy says, "I'm serious. Shaving down there is dangerous. Especially your balls."

"Why?"

She gives him a look. "Are you sure you want to hear this at lunch?"

"I can take it. Please: proceed with your lecture."

"Very well. The skin on your scrotum is filled with folds and wrinkles, which trap enormous quantities of bacteria. Every time you shave you're risking a cut. And even the smallest cut can result in bacterial infection."

"Which is why they make antibiotics."

"Yes, and that's fine, provided you don't wind up with Fournier gangrene."

"What's that?"

"Flesh eating bacteria on your balls."

"Whoa!"

"It can happen, believe me. And if it's not caught in time it can kill you. And if it is, you know how they fix it?"

"Tell me."

"They have to surgically remove all the skin from your balls."

"Jesus!"

"Exactly. So, stop shaving your balls, Bobby. Ever done prison time?"

"Excuse me?"

"It's a simple question."

"Are you talking about prison time or jail time?"

"Either."

"Both."

She does a double-take. "Really?"

He nods.

"What did you do?"

"Hired a bad lawyer."

"You can't go to prison for hiring a bad lawyer."

"You can if you kill him."

Her eyes go big. "You killed your *attorney?*"

"Accidentally. He was strangling my mother at the time, and I hit him. I didn't realize he had a brain tumor."

"Why was he strangling her?"

"He found out she was sleeping with men for money, and it didn't sit well since he'd bought her a house."

"Your lawyer was your mother's boyfriend?"

"Fiancé. So anyway, they sentenced me to 31 months in Angola for involuntary manslaughter, but I only served two weeks."

"How'd you manage that?"

"Hours after my sentencing, the prosecuting attorney was caught falsifying evidence in two cases that took place years earlier. So, the state vacated all his convictions, starting with the most recent, which was mine."

"Lucky you. How much money do you need?"

"For what?"

"Your dream. I mean, you obviously have some sort of master plan, or you wouldn't be offering your ass for eleven bucks an hour. What are you working toward? What's your dream?"

"You'll laugh."

"Probably, but tell me anyway."

"I want to own the #1 tourist destination in the state."

"Based on your artifact?"

"Yeah, but that's just one item. I've already got dozens more, waiting to be certified."

"Tell me about the one you have."

"It's something you need to see."

"Why?"

"It's one-of-a-kind."

"Where is it?"

"In my trailer."

She gives him a look.

He says, "I'm not a rapist, or anything."

"Or *anything*? What does *that* mean?"

"It means I'm not dangerous."

She eats another fry before saying, "I think you *are* dangerous. Because not once have you asked about the guy I was hiding from this morning, and that tells me you're not afraid of him."

"Should I be?"

She holds his gaze several seconds. "How long does it take to get to your place?"

"From here? Fifteen minutes. Why?"

"I never thought these words would come out of my mouth, but... take me to your trailer, Bobby. Show me your shrine."

Chapter 3

AFTER BOBBY PAYS the bill, Daisy follows him in her rental car past Billeaud, onto 96, and half-way to St. Martinville, where he abruptly turns left onto a gravel road that leads to a broken-down trailer park where she notices something she's heard about but never seen: laundry hanging on clotheslines. When she parks her car beside his and climbs out, a hard-looking woman approaches Bobby and says, "This has to stop."

"What does?"

"My girls gettin' fat. It can't go on."

"It's just two or three bites."

"Times twenty-four, times four days a week. And they're *swallowin'* them bites. Bottom line, it's over. We're done. Come get your shit." She looks at Daisy. "Who're you?"

"Daisy Pepper."

"*Pepper?*"

Daisy nods.

"You a movie star?"

"No ma'am."

"Yes you are, you're Emma Roberts! I'd know you anywhere. You could be covered in mud, you'd still be Emma."

"I'm truly not," Daisy says, "but thanks for the compliment."

"Where you from?"

"Cincinnati."

"I mean, where were you born? And don't tell me it weren't Rhinebeck, New York, famous for arts and culture and tree-lined streets and charmin' bed and breakfasts where you can rest your head on feather pillows after a relaxin' day of stress-free shoppin' in specialty boutiques."

Daisy's eyes grow large. "How did you *know?*"

"Same way I know your birthday's February 10, 1991. You're Emma Roberts."

Daisy looks around, then whispers, "You can't tell anyone."

"Your secret's safe with me, Emma. And I won't even *ask* what you're doin' hangin' out with *this* low-life piece of trash, 'less you're scoutin' locations for a hillbilly movie or lookin' for his wayward brother, Jake. And if so, he ain't here. Ain't stepped *foot* on this dung pile since their mama died, Lord rest her soul."

Bobby says, "I'll fetch the product in twenty minutes."

"Make it five. And bring cash, this time."

She starts to leave, then looks at Daisy and says, "Why'd you shuck your duds in that movie we rented last week at the Red Box?"

"It was essential for moving the plot forward."

"Essential, huh?"

"Yes, ma'am."

"Well, it set my girls into a strippin' frenzy. They raced through the VFW in their underpants till Mindy Theriot took it to a whole new level and showed both sides of her privates to a room full of colonels." She furrows her brows with disapproval. "You need to be aware of the consequences your movies have on normal folk."

"I'm sorry. Is Mindy okay?"

"She is now, but it took two exorcisms, and the priest says if she don't get another one by middle school she'll be the queen slut in high school, just like her ma. Did Bobby tell you about my Girl Scouts?"

"No ma'am."

"Don't be stupid, young lady."

"Excuse me?"

"Don't get caught up in his vortex. Get in your car, drive back to Hollywood, and put this man in your rear-view mirror. He ain't right in the head."

"Are you referring to his shrine?"

"I'm referrin' to the whole damn deal!" She turns at the sound of tires on gravel 50 yards behind them. "Speakin' of which, it appears you got a fresh car full of rubes. I s'pect you'll want Sadie, am I right?"

"Please," Bobby says. "But call them True Believers, not rubes."

"Whatever. Emma?"

"Yes, ma'am?"

"I warned you, girl."

"You did. Thank you."

"Keep your damn clothes on!"

"Yes, ma'am."

"Agnes."

"Ma'am?"

"That's my name. I'll be back in a minute."

Before greeting his customers, Bobby whispers, "Are you really Emma Roberts?"

"You're joking, right?"

He says, "I never banged a movie star before."

"There's a shock."

"No A-listers, anyway."

Though he has no clue who Emma Roberts is, Bobby stares at her face till the True Believers spill out of their car. Then he turns to them and says:

Chapter 4

"FRIENDS, PLEASE GATHER 'round. I'm Bobby Cujo, and—" He puts his hand over his heart and adds: "I'm humbled by your visit. I know you traveled a great distance to be here today, and rest assured, your sacrifice is about to be rewarded beyond your wildest dreams. You are literally three steps and a doorway from a glimpse of heaven."

"That's mighty big talk," a man says.

"Right you are, sir! May I ask *you* a question?"

The man shrugs.

"Could it be you're a genius? Or a prophet?"

"I don't reckon that's likely."

"Well, you may be both and don't know it yet, because the good Lord works on His timetable, not ours."

"Amen!" a woman says.

Bobby adds, "But you're right about big talk: it sneaks around the corner to take a piss whenever Truth shows up, am I right?"

"I wouldn't know."

"Exactly! And that's my point: you've been told all your life there are a million different types of people in the world, but in truth, there are only two: those who've *seen* my artifact...and those who haven't.

So today you need to decide which type you're gonna be. Will you travel this far only to change your mind at the last minute, content to live your life ignorant of the divine power that lies beyond that hallowed door? Or will you be one of the precious, sacred few who'll live their remaining years in the blessed, happy knowledge they've seen the artifact? Before you answer, consider this: *anyone* can say they've *never* seen it. But today, only *you* have a chance to tell your friends and neighbors that you *have*."

"How much does it cost?"

"Well, that's a good question, and it delights me to announce how pitifully small the contribution is: the *total* cost...including tax... is only five thousand dollars."

"*What?*"

"I'm only kidding, Sir! It's just five dollars."

"Five *dollars?*"

"That's correct."

"To see a *Moon Pie?* Are you *crazy?* You can buy all the Moon Pies you want for a dollar!"

"*Sir?*"

"What?"

"Are you aware the Chattanooga Bakery, of Chattanooga, Tennessee has been making Moon Pies every single day since April 29th, 1917?"

"So?"

"They manufacture a million Moon Pies a *day*. That's 365 million Moon Pies every *year!*"

"So?"

"How many of those Moon Pies do you suppose are the perfect image of John the Baptist?"

"I have no idea."

"Well, the answer is...just one. And it's on display right behind me. Friends, your wretched existence is over. Now, all that stands between you and the greatest bliss you'll ever experience...is a single piece of paper: a five dollar bill."

The "Amen!" woman says, "I heard some girl took three bites out of it."

"Absolutely correct, Ma'am, and an angel of a girl she is, with a name so sweet and pure it softens the hardest heart just to utter it in public, and so I shall: Norma Grace Tully, of Labadieville, Louisiana. A Daisy Scout, and true believer in all things righteous and holy." He looks carefully at the three couples before saying, "If any of you are currently cheating on your spouses I can't accept your contribution. While it's not my place to judge, I simply cannot permit you to cast your eyes on the product of Norma Grace's divine culinary intervention."

"Do we get a couple's discount?" another woman asks.

"If only I could offer it," Bobby says. "But the greatest part of your contribution goes to the local chapter of Girl Scouts. As I said, Norma Grace is a Daisy, but my shrine benefits both Daisy *and* Brownie Scouts in the local area. If it were just me, I'd let you see this amazing artifact for free, and more than once, because it would be my honor to allow the healing powers of John the Baptist to wash over you and cleanse your soul and change your lives for the better. But that wouldn't be fair to the children, who depend on your contributions to continue their paths to adulthood under the caring, watchful eyes of devoted scout mothers throughout the parish. With that said, I'll ask you now: which of you—who are not currently cheating on your spouse—are ready to part with a mere five dollars in order to view this amazing spectacle?"

No one steps forward.

Bobby waits.

"I might have to pass," one man says, finally. He and his wife turn and start to walk away.

Bobby shouts: "Sir: wait! What if you could meet Norma Grace Tully in person? The very girl who once sat on the front steps of Saint Philomena Catholic Church in Coventry, Louisiana, and took three precious bites of the Moon Pie her sainted mother packed for her field trip that famous morning?"

They turn around. "Is she *here*?"

Bobby shows them a triumphant smile. "She is!"

"Well, in *that* case..."

Bobby collects the money and stuffs it in his pocket. Then says: "Norma Grace is currently at the VFW Hall, inspiring her fellow scouts. But I anticipated your desire to see her and sent a messenger to fetch her even as you were parking your car. In short, she'll be here directly. While you wait, can I interest anyone in an ice-cold Dr. Pepper for only a dollar?"

He collects their orders and pulls six Dr. Peppers from a massive cooler. Moments later Agnes ambles toward the group, dragging a dirty little girl dressed in a Daisy Scout uniform behind her.

"That's *Norma Grace*?" one of the women asks.

Bobby nods. Then says, "Agnes, would you please make the introductions?"

"I'm Agnes Gauthiereaux," she says, "and this here's Norma Grace Tully, of Labadieville, Louisiana, who's visiting our scout troop this week. I apologize for her appearance, but the girls were in the middle of a scrimmage when Brother Cujo asked me to fetch her."

"What type of scrimmage?"

"Football."

"This tiny child plays football?"

"Why not?" Bobby says. "This *is* Louisiana, after all."

When Agnes releases Grace's hand, the little girl falls to her knees and delivers a heart-wrenching prayer for the visitors. After answering several questions: yes, she bit into the Moon Pie; no, she had no idea how significant it was till she saw it glowing under the light of a halo; yes, it has the power to heal people, including her grandma, who—after years of suffering—is now cancer-free...the men and women touch her shoulder and Agnes leads her back to wherever they came from. Then the six guests and Daisy enter Bobby's musty trailer and gaze upon the John the Baptist Moon Pie, which Bobby keeps on an elevated cake plate, under glass, atop a wooden box covered in crushed velvet. The men fall to their knees and start testifying, and the women raise their hands skyward, offering up an assortment of celestial bench presses.

After they leave, Daisy shakes her head. "*This* is what you do for a living?"

He grins.

"You can't *possibly* make any money from it."

"Last year I cleared six grand. Tax-free, I might add."

"How's it tax-free?"

He winks. "I don't report it."

Daisy says, "Now I know what Donald Trump would be doing if he hadn't inherited two hundred million bucks."

"Omigod!"

"What?"

"I can't believe I'm falling in love with a *Hillary* voter! Shit! Although I should've seen it coming since Yankees always vote for Yankees."

"Trump's a Yankee."

"Not when he's in Florida. And that's the beauty of the man. I mean, do you have any idea what it's like for him? After all these years to finally be in the White House where he can do what he always wanted to do?"

"What, legally evict a black family?"

He starts to say something, then stops. "You're talking about the Obamas?" He chuckles. "Actually, that's pretty funny. Where was I?"

"Last year you cleared six grand, tax-free."

"Right. I know it don't sound like much, but if a single Moon Pie can generate six grand, guess what 100 would be worth?"

Daisy waits for him to say. When he doesn't, she guesses: "*Seven* grand?"

"Try $600,000!"

She laughs.

He says, "You clearly have no idea how these things work."

"Clearly."

"But assume for a minute I'm right. What's your first thought?"

"You're gonna need a bigger trailer."

"Exactly!"

"So how do you intend to acquire the other 99 artifacts?"

"That's where Agnes comes in. At this very moment, eight little Girl Scouts are taking random bites out of Moon Pies at the VFW. In a little while, I'll collect them and see if any happen to resemble the ancient prophets. With any luck, I'll get a Virgin Mary, and two or three wise men for the manger scene I aim to have by Christmas."

"How many Moon Pies are those poor children consuming?"

"Ninety-six a week. But don't pay attention to Agnes. Every week she threatens to quit, but she's come to depend on the hundred a month I pay her." He pauses. "Do you see yourself in this picture?"

"Which picture is that?"

"The religious artifact business. As my partner."

"Are you for real?"

"Imagine what you and I could do if we pool our resources and start working together."

"Dude, I'm just passing through. I've got my own shit to deal with."

He looks at her. "What do *you* do for a living?"

"You won't believe me."

"Try me."

"My profession is molecular bioscience, and my specialty is calliotoxins. My subject of choice is the blue coral snake."

"*Blue* corals? You sure about that?"

"Quite."

"Well, we've got plenty of coral snakes, but I never saw nor heard of a *blue* one."

"Like me, they're not from around here. They're indigenous to the area between Bangkok and Peninsular Malaysia."

"Bangkok?"

"That's right."

Bobby grins. "Confucius say: 'Man who walk through broken turnstile at bus station going to Bangkok.'"

"Just so you know, your accent is both racist and degrading."

"Lighten up, Hillary Girl. Confucius also say: 'Man with hole in pocket gonna feel cocky all day.'"

"Are you done?"

"For now. Why do you study blue corals?"

"They're the only snakes in the world whose venom targets sodium channels."

"I have no idea what that means."

"It blocks nerve impulses within seconds. I'm hoping my studies will lead to the development of a synthetic, non-narcotic painkiller."

"What would that be worth?"

"Billions."

"Holy shit! Who's paying you to do the study?"

"Right now? No one. But I have high hopes."

"So how are you supporting yourself?"

"I make pizzas. From scratch."

He grins. "You're a *baker*?"

"Used to be."

"You know what Confucius said about bakers?"

"No. But I *do* know your jokes are highly offensive."

He hangs his head.

She says, "Go ahead and tell it. I know you're dying to. But just this once. Then, never again."

He chuckles, then says, "Confucius say: 'Man who put cream in tart not always a baker.'"

She frowns. "That was even worse than I expected."

He says, "Would you like to know what's *really* going on between you and me right now?"

"Tell me," Daisy says.

Chapter 5

"I THINK FATE brought us together," Bobby says. "You lost your job, and here you are. This is your true destiny."

Daisy laughs. "Save your breath, con man. I don't believe that spiritual shit. Not to mention, your Moon Pie story's got more holes in it than an Alabama road sign."

"What do you mean?"

"For starters, no one knows what John the Baptist looked like. They didn't have cameras back then, remember? Second, it's a fucking cookie, not a religious artifact. Third, that little waif you presented as Norma Grace might be adorable, but she's a complete phony, which means you're using a minor to defraud the public. Why are you smiling?"

"Because you have no idea how cute you are right now."

"Don't change the subject. You said the Chattanooga Bakery has made Moon Pies every day since April 29th, 1917."

"So?"

"April 29th, 1917 was a Sunday. Are you telling me they started making Moon Pies on a Sunday and kept doing so all these years?"

"I don't know. I mean, I got that off their website, so..."

"You said Norma Grace ate her Moon Pie while sitting on the front steps of Saint Philomena Catholic Church in Coventry, Louisiana."

"So?"

"There *are* no front steps at that particular church."

"How do you *know* all that?"

"I looked it up on my phone while you were giving your spiel. I also verified—to my extreme shock—that your Moon Pie *is*, in fact, certified as an official religious shrine. How'd you manage that?"

"Same way car companies get to be the official cars of the Super Bowl."

"You paid a fee?"

He nods.

"Agnes said you had a brother."

"So?"

"Where is he?"

"I'd rather talk about us."

"What's there to talk about?"

"You've got me all worked up." He points to the bulge in his crotch. "You've seen the *before* version. I guarantee you're gonna *love* the *after!*"

"How about we save that for my nightmares."

"Why?"

"My husband passed away recently. I'm not ready for sex yet."

"You were *married?*"

"That's how it works, Bobby: you can't have a husband without being married."

"What happened to him?"

"He was murdered."

"How?"

"I'd rather not talk about it."

"When was this?"

"Couple months ago."

Bobby sighs. "That's awful, Daisy. It truly is." He pauses a moment, then says, "But you know what I think? I think your husband would want you to get on with your life."

"You think he'd want me to fuck you, huh?"

He smiles. "You already said you found me attractive. And anyway, I think we might be soul mates."

"Based on what?"

In one quick motion, he pulls his pants and underwear to his ankles and steps out of them, points to his dick and says: "This."

While it's in Daisy's nature to throw shade whenever possible, the sheer volume of what he's placed before her short-circuits her brain, and causes but two words to escape her lips: "Holy shit!"

With two quick steps, Bobby closes the distance between them, embraces her, and kisses her on the mouth. When she doesn't stop him or pull away, he says, "I swear to God you're the prettiest woman I've ever kissed."

"Thank you."

He kisses her again with great feeling, then turns her around, slides his hand under her shirt and bra and finds a nipple. As Daisy's eyes roll up into her head, Bobby pinches it ever-so-lightly and tugs it gently with his fingertips till it's erect and hard as a pencil eraser. Then he cups her breast and rolls his palm over it, grasping and lifting and working it from the base up, as if kneading pizza dough after the second fermentation. After a few moments, he moves his hand downward over her taut belly and slides it under her jeans till he feels the soft hair spilling from the upper edge of her panties. As he angles his arm to work his way lower she says, "Oh hey, Bobby?"

"Yeah?"

"Before you get too busy down there, there's something I need to tell you."

"Can it wait?"

"I wouldn't think so."

"Well, whatever it is, it won't affect this raging hard-on."

"I think it might."

She unbuttons her jeans and lowers the zipper. "Can you move your hand please?"

"Seriously?"

"Yes please."

"But I'm *dying* here."

"Just for a minute."

He sighs, removes his hand. "Tampon?"

"Not exactly." She turns to face him. "I don't want to freak you out, but every morning I put my dead husband's wedding ring in my vagina to remind me of his sacred memory."

Bobby backs up a step. While he considers her comment at least two sandwiches shy of a picnic, he knows better than to make negative comments when he's *this close* to new pussy. Shamelessly, he says, "I've heard of widows doing that. It's quite touching, actually."

Daisy says, "If we're really gonna do this, I need to remove it."

"Okay."

She reaches inside her panties. "May I place it on the table?"

"Sure. Table's fine. Whatever."

It's only when Daisy places the ring on the table that Bobby realizes it's attached to a severed finger. His reaction is both sudden and predictable: he passes out. And when he comes to, she's holding a gun in his face.

"Last chance," she says. "Where's your brother?"

Chapter 6

"WHAT ARE YOU *doing?*" Bobby says.

"Asking a question that requires a life-or-death answer: Where's Jake Cujo?"

He takes a moment to gather his equilibrium. Then says, "Look. I've got ice cold beer in the fridge. How about we relax, have a beer, talk this out?"

"How about you answer my question?"

Bobby smiles. "You're not gonna shoot me."

Daisy cocks the hammer to convince him otherwise, but he looks behind her and says, "Is that the guy you were hiding from this morning?"

She laughs. "This isn't the movies, Bobby. I'm not gonna turn my head and let you overpower me."

But the voice behind her says, "Drop the gun, Buttercup."

Five minutes later she and Bobby are tied to chairs in the minuscule dining area while the intruder presses keys on Bobby's phone and computer.

"Who the fuck are *you?*" Bobby says.

"Tony, from Miami."

Daisy says, "You tied us up while searching his computer? Omigod, that's like the oldest cliché in the book."

"You'd like to think so," Tony says, "but *this* book is only six chapters in."

Before Daisy has time to roll her eyes, a second man enters the trailer and says, "Bunch of kids headin' this way."

Tony says, "Jeez, Eddie. You're scared of *kids?*"

"No, but I'm not gonna *shoot* 'em."

"Why not?"

"I only got six bullets."

"How many kids?"

"Eight."

"Well, if you shoot the first six I bet the others'll scatter."

Eddie says, "You're shittin' me, right?"

Tony hands him his gun. "Now you got twelve bullets. No excuses."

Eddie shrugs, starts to leave.

"Wait!" Bobby says. "Whatever you're looking for, just tell me. I'll give it to you."

"Can't afford to be seen by the kids."

"If you stay inside and lock the door I'll trick them into stealing some sodas and running away."

Eddie closes the door, locks it, looks at Bobby. "You know you're sitting there bare-assed, right?" He notices the ring on the counter and says, "What the *fuck?*"

By then the Girl Scouts are banging on the trailer door. One yells, "We know you're in there, Bobby! Come out."

"Go home!" Bobby shouts.

"We ain't been paid and we're out of Moon Pies. Give us another case or we're gonna eat the ones we bit."

"I can't. I'm tied up at the moment."

Now Daisy rolls her eyes.

Tony motions Bobby to move things along, so he hollers, "Look, I'm all out of Moon Pies, but don't you *dare* eat the ones you bit. And whatever you do, don't touch those Dr. Peppers in the cooler, or I'll skin you alive."

A tiny voice giggles. "We're *already* alive! Fuck *you*, Bobby Cujo!"

Eddie peers out the window.

Tony says, "What're they doing?"

"Like he said: stealin' his sodas and runnin' away. I probably shoulda shot 'em."

"It's not too late."

"They're just kids," Daisy says.

"*Kids?* That one little shit just yelled 'fuck you!'"

"They're on a sugar high."

As Eddie studies the severed finger, Bobby asks, "What do you *want?*"

Tony points at Daisy. "Same thing *she* wants: your brother."

"Why?"

And Tony says:

Chapter 7

"HE OWES US money."

"I doubt that."

"See?" Tony says to Eddie. "This is what happens when you engage 'em in conversation. It's the reason I always used to punch 'em in the mouth till they told me what I wanted to know."

"So, punch him already," Eddie says.

"Here's my problem with that: remember that last guy I punched? I fractured my hand. Time before that? I dislocated a knuckle."

"You ain't doin' it right."

Tony laughs. "I know how to *do* it, asshole. I been *doin'* it all my life. The problem's the angle: when they're sittin' down, tied up, the angle's all wrong. Plus, I found out the hard way it ain't smart to hit 'em in the head *regardless* of the angle."

"That's bullshit! I hit 'em in the head all the time."

"That just means you've been lucky. Problem is, heads ain't just hard, they also got sharp ridges you can't see under a guy's hair. Better to punch him in the nose, or mouth."

"Then do it."

"Again, the problem's the angle. You punch downward on a guy's nose or mouth hard enough, you might break his tooth. You cut your hand on that broken tooth, you got major problems."

"Like what?"

Daisy says, "It could result in a serious infection and permanent nerve damage."

Eddie says, "Who asked *you*?"

"I'm just trying to be helpful. I took a college course on human saliva. Can I tell you what I learned?"

"No."

"Tell *me*," Tony says.

"Human saliva contains more than 100,000 microorganisms, including 200 species of bacteria. Punching people's faces is like playing Russian Roulette: it only takes one mistake to make you a cripple."

"Thanks, Buttercup. You were me, how would you do it?"

"I'd use a weapon."

Tony grins. "I like this girl."

Eddie says, "I know what she's hopin' for. I hit a guy with my gun once, and it fired a shot. I barely got outta the house in time."

"Doesn't have to be a gun," Daisy says. "In college, I beat a guy half to death with a bar of soap."

"Bullshit!" Tony says.

Eddie asks, "How'd you do it?"

"I waited till he fell asleep, then put a bar of soap in a sock, climbed on top of him, and whaled away."

"You hit him like that while he was sound *asleep*? That's harsh."

"He deserved it."

"What'd he *do*?"

"What do you *think*?"

Tony stares at her a moment, then says, "We're gettin' sidetracked. Yo, Bobby: where's Jake hidin'?"

"I haven't seen him in over a year."

"Let's call him."

"We can't. He uses burner phones. I don't have any of the numbers."

"Why not? You're his brother."

"We're not close."

"Where does he live?"

"Outside Madisonville, on the Tchefuncte River."

Tony takes his phone from his pocket and presses a couple of buttons. "How you spell that?"

"I don't know, and neither does anyone else. But it doesn't matter, 'cause there's no address. It's just a fishing shack on the river."

"How far from here?"

"Two hours, forty minutes."

Tony takes a deep breath, lets it out slowly. "I guess we got ourselves a road trip."

Eddie says, "What're we gonna do with these two?"

"Take 'em with us."

"Why?"

"How else are we gonna find a fishin' shack on a river no one can spell?"

Daisy says, "Bobby? Aren't you forgetting something?"

"What?"

"This is the part where you're supposed to say, 'I'll take you to my brother, but only if you let Daisy go.'"

"Why would I say that?"

"Because you're a good guy, and it's the right thing to do."

"Are you *kidding*! Ten minutes ago, you were gonna *shoot* me!"

"No, I wasn't. I was just acting tough. I don't even know how to shoot a gun."

Tony says, "How about it, Bobby? Want us to let her go?"

"Hell no!"

"Why not?"

"If you let her go, I'll never see her again."

"No shit you won't!" Tony says, laughing.

Daisy frowns. "See what I'm up against?"

Eddie looks at Tony. "*Would* you have let her go?"

"Fuck no. But I gotta agree with Buttercup. What type of asshole wouldn't at least *ask?*"

Eddie says, "If we're takin' a car ride I'll require food and drinks. What's he got?"

"There's beer in the fridge," Tony says. "I didn't see much else, besides that half-eaten Moon Pie on the cake plate."

"Where's that?"

Tony points to it.

"No!" Bobby shouts, but Eddie ignores him, lifts the glass, grabs the Moon Pie, takes a bite...and promptly cracks two teeth. As he hollers, Tony removes two beers from the fridge and starts rummaging through the kitchen drawers, looking for a bottle opener. Eddie punches the top of Bobby's head full force and immediately regrets it. As the blood seeps from his cut hand he shouts, "*Damn* it!"

"We tried to warn you," Daisy says.

"You fuckin' *jinxed* me!"

Enraged, Eddie pushes Bobby backward onto the floor, stands over him, calls him a motherfucker, punches him repeatedly with his good hand, and kicks him in the ribs several times for good measure. By then the beer bottles are open, and Tony's indulging. Eddie goes to the sink, puts his mouth under the faucet, and allows the cool water to run over his sore teeth. Then he swishes some water in his mouth, spits it out, and turns his attention to his hand. He washes the cut with dishwashing soap, then rinses it, and dries it with a paper towel. Then he grabs the remaining beer and starts chugging.

Five minutes later, both men are puking their guts out. After another five minutes, they're on the floor, dead.

"What's going on?" Daisy says.

Through swollen, bloody lips Bobby says: "This is the part where you're supposed to say, 'Are you okay, Bobby?'"

"I'd act more concerned if you'd begged them to set me free, which you did not."

"I keep poisoned beer in the fridge."

"*What?*"

"In case anyone tries to steal my artifact."

"You *bastard!*"

"What are you *talking* about? I just saved your *life!*"

"You offered *me* one of those beers!"

"If we're being technical," Bobby says, "you were threatening to shoot me at the time."

"I still plan to."

It suddenly dawns on them that the first one to get free gets the guns.

Chapter 8

THEY START WRIGGLING and thrashing and throwing themselves around, but Tony obviously knew what he was doing when he tied them, and thirty minutes later, they're both on their backs on the floor, side-by-side, completely exhausted, no closer to being free.

"Now what?" Daisy says.

"Are you really planning to shoot me?"

"No."

"Why are you looking for my brother?"

"It's complicated."

"How much do you know about him?"

She was about to say "nothing," then decides to offer this much: "He consorts with criminals and was the last person seen with my sister, Julie."

"Is she dead?"

"Missing. And Jake had something to do with it."

"I don't believe that."

"I know it for a fact."

"You've got the wrong guy. Jake wouldn't hurt a young woman. Especially not a pretty one."

"Who said she's pretty?"

"She's *your* sister, isn't she?"

A brief smile crosses Daisy's face, then fades. "Four days ago, a guy named Joey Zorba told me the whole story."

"Joey lied."

"I don't think so, 'cause he had an ice pick in his chest at the time, and wanted to confess his crimes before dying. He said he killed Jake's partner, a guy named Sully. He also said Jake was involved in Julie's disappearance."

Bobby looks skeptical. "He said all that with an icepick in his chest?"

"Yup."

"And he specifically fingered *Jake?*"

"No. He specifically fingered *me*, which is how he wound up with an ice pick in his chest."

"What're you, some sort of bad ass?"

"No, but my boyfriend is."

"Who's your boyfriend?"

"Vinny dePazzio."

"Never heard of him," Bobby says, but the name sounds familiar. When it finally registers, he sputters. "Holy shit! You don't mean the *gangster!* Vinny the *Prick?*"

"You've heard of him?"

"He's your *boyfriend?*"

"Not by choice."

They're quiet till Bobby says, "Am I in danger?"

She laughs. "Let's think it through: In the last hour, you poisoned two mob guys and tried to fuck Vinny the Prick's girlfriend. What do *you* think?"

"Shit! I *knew* you were too good to be true!"

"Consider it a teaching moment on the weakness of men: whether you're the president of a major corporation or a low-life conman you're all the same: you wouldn't take a man's phone call without running a credit report, but you'll jump into bed with his wife or daughter without a second thought."

"How'd it happen?"

"What are we talking about?"

"How'd you wind up with Vinny the Prick?"

"He fell in love with my pizzas."

"I'm being serious right now, Daisy."

"Me too. Vinny's goons used to order pizza from my dad's shop. One day he tasted my Margherita—that's a type of pizza, not what you're thinking—and went crazy. So, he came to the shop to meet my dad and found out I'm the one who makes the pies. After that, he dropped in every day to flirt, and every day I turned him down and my dad started complaining about it, so Vinny bought the store and forced my dad into retirement. When my sister went missing I flew to New Orleans and tried to find her. I went up and down the streets showing her picture, handing out fliers, kept harassing the cops...and of course without me there, the store fell apart. Vinny said if I came back to work and became his girlfriend he'd use his connections to find Julie and bring her back."

"And you did?"

"I had no other choice."

"I don't believe a word of it. Nor do I believe Jake had anything to do with Julie's disappearance."

"Jake sells storage containers, right?"

"He *used* to, till he sold the company."

"Well, apparently, he sold the company to Joey Zorba. And you know where Joey got the money to buy it?"

"He borrowed it from Vinny?"

"No. Vinny's in charge of the Northeast mob. Joey probably borrowed the money from Rocco Tucci, who runs the *Southeast* mob. After Joey died, Rocco must've sold his debt to *these* goons, and told them to keep making the payments. You heard what Tony said, right? That Jake owes him money? They need Jake to run the business, and he skipped out on them. Any more questions?"

"Yeah. Is that really your husband's ring and severed finger?"

"No. It's a fake."

"The finger?"

"The ring." She pauses. "Look at your face. I'm joking!"

"So, you've never been married?"

"Nope. But I slip the ring and fake finger in my panties when I'm in situations where I could be compromised, like a bar, or a weird guy's trailer in South Louisiana. You wouldn't believe how helpful it's been, keeping assholes at bay."

"Actually, I *would*," Bobby says. Then his voice goes solemn. "So, this whole thing with me was a setup?" He sighs. "I'm such an idiot. All this time I thought you liked me."

"Don't pout," she says. "Of *course* I like you! I let you feel me up, didn't I?"

"I guess. Look: are you telling the truth about this Joey Zorba guy?"

"More or less."

He shakes his head. "Are you at least positive Julie's missing?"

"If she weren't, she would've called me."

"Just because she hasn't called doesn't mean—"

"We're not like you and Jake. We're extremely close. We talked every day. Trust me, she's missing."

Bobby wants to ask, "What proof do you have that Jake was involved?" But can't, because one of the dead guys has suddenly come back to life.

Chapter 9

THE NOT-SO-DEAD TONY speaks with a raspy, guttural voice that emanates from deep within his throat: "You *poisoned* me?"

"It was an accident," Daisy says. "A misunderstanding."

Tony raises his head and coughs up a quart of bile so thick it slaps the trailer floor like a wet sheet. He gives them a hard look, but his heart's not in it, and when he speaks, his eyes roll up in his head and his voice gets softer with each word: "I...will...fuckin'...kill...you both!"

He attempts to stand, but lurches, slams into the kitchen cabinets, slips on his vomit slick and falls back to the floor.

Daisy says, "When you get a minute, do you think you could untie me?"

"Fuck you."

"That's unacceptable."

Tony laughs, which turns out to be a mistake because even though Daisy knows that laughter can trigger the release of endorphins that help the body regulate pain, it's also a fundamentally physical activity that forces the diaphragm, abdomen, back, shoulders, and 15 facial muscles to spasm and contract, and when you've been poisoned like

Tony, the endorphins don't mean shit. You're gonna do what Tony does: scream in agony.

"Vinny dePazzio would expect you to untie me," she says.

"Yeah, well Vinny ain't here," he groans, then passes out for ten minutes. When he comes to, he's much improved, though still too weak to stand. Content to sit in a pool of his own vomit for the time being, Tony stares at his dead colleague a couple minutes before saying, "Wait. You know Vinny?"

And then it hits him. "You're Vinny's new girl! From the pizza parlor."

"That's right."

"The fuck're you doin' *here?*"

"Looking for Jake Cujo."

"Why do *you* want him?"

"He kidnapped my sister. If you can pull yourself together, maybe we can help each other."

"Vinny knows you're here?"

"No. So don't tell him."

"Why the fuck would *I* talk to him? I work for Rocco. But this much I know: it ain't wise to withhold details from Vinny. They don't call him Vinny the Prick for nothin'. He's a mean mother-fucker."

"He's all that and a bucket of piss," Daisy says. "But that's not why they call him Vinny the Prick. It's because of his dick."

"How big is it?"

"Just the opposite. You could fit it inside your pinkie finger and have enough space left over for three skittles."

He looks at his pinkie and chuckles, then winces and says, "You gotta stop makin' me laugh." He takes a moment to compose himself. "Swear to God that's where he got the nickname?"

"Yeah. And the reason he likes it is because people think it means he's a rat bastard, or he has a big dick, or both."

"But it's tiny, right?"

Daisy says, "I'm gonna tell you something you won't believe, but I swear it's true. You know that ring on the counter? The one with the fake finger?"

"Yeah?"

"On the night Vinny claimed to have the biggest boner of his life I slipped it on his dick like a cock ring, and when he climbed on top of me it slid right off and fell on my stomach."

Tony howls with laughter, and screams from it as well.

"Okay," he says. "I'll help you get loose. But I expect a blow job."

"Of course. How about it, Bobby: you'll take care of Tony, won't you?"

Tony says, "From *you*, not him. We got a deal? You'll never get loose otherwise."

Daisy sighs. "I guess so."

"Yes or no?"

"Yes."

Bobby says, "Are you *kidding* me? You're gonna *blow* this guy? How easy *are* you, anyway?"

Daisy narrows her eyes. "*Really*, Bobby? I'm *easy*? If I were blowing *you* instead of Tony you'd be all over it. You'd be calling me sweetheart, and take all the credit for being such a stud."

"At least you and me have a history."

"*History*? I've known you exactly two hours longer than I've known Tony!"

"Fine. Blow him. Go ahead and fuck him while you're at it. I don't give a shit."

"Yeah, okay, Bobby. 'Cause that's what I've been waiting for: your permission."

"Fuck you!"

"Sorry, not gonna happen. I'm Tony's girl, remember?"

"Shut up, both of you!" Tony says. "You're givin' me a headache."

Chapter 10

ON SHAKY LEGS, Tony makes his way to Bobby's knife drawer, selects a chef's knife, and holds it up.

Daisy says, "Unless you intend to kill me, put that away and use a boning knife if he has one."

"What's it look like?"

"Small, flexible, with a curved blade."

He rummages around, then holds one up. "Is this it?"

"Yes. Thank you."

Imitating Daisy's voice, he mutters: "*Use a boning knife, if he has one.*" Now, cutting her loose, he says, "Your wrists are bleeding." He looks at Bobby. "His too. You must've struggled hard." He chuckles. "Waste of time. You would've stayed tied till you died."

Daisy says, "Where'd you learn to tie like that?"

"My grandfather."

"What was he, a fisherman?"

"Stage Magician." Then, with pride, adds: "And former Executive Director of the IGKT."

"What's that?"

"The International Guild of Knot Tyers."

"You're shitting us, right?" Bobby says.

"You're not even *in* this conversation, asshole."

"But you're gonna untie me, aren't you?"

"No."

"Why not?"

"It's easier to beat the shit outta you if you're tied up."

"You don't need to work me over. I'll take you to my brother's place."

"The trip to your brother's is why you're still alive. The beatin's for killin' Eddie."

"You can't possibly believe Daisy's gonna blow you..."

As Tony cuts the last strand of rope he says, "She'd better, 'cause we made a deal and I expect her to stick to it. Like she said, Vinny don't know she's here. If she winds up dead in a Louisiana swamp, he won't know who put her there. How 'bout it, Buttercup? You gonna stand by your promise, or am I gonna have to get rough with you?"

"I'm insulted you felt the need to ask me that," Daisy says, rubbing her wrists. "But would you consider showering first?"

"No, I would not."

"Well, would you at least remove all your soiled clothing out here, and let me blow you in the bedroom? Because it's one thing to make me gag; quite another to make me vomit."

"That's fair."

"Thank you."

Bobby watches Tony strip, watches him and Daisy enter the bedroom, watches them close the door. Moments later he hears a gasp, then a long period of quiet. When the door finally opens and Daisy walks out, he says: "Proud of yourself?"

"Yeah, but you're gonna need some new sheets."

"Why? Because you don't swallow?"

"Don't be gross, Bobby."

"What's Tony doing?"

"Lying peacefully."

"With a smile on his face? I can only imagine."

"Actually, he's dead."

"*What?*"

"I strangled him."

"*How?*"

"He was 80% dead when we walked in the room. I'm only 110 pounds, but it's more weight on his chest than he could handle in that condition."

"So, you *didn't* blow him?"

She frowns. "Can you really think so little of me?"

"I barely know you. Why do I need new sheets? Did he vomit again?"

"Worse: he shit himself. But we've got a bigger problem right now."

"Like what?"

She walks across the room, stands above him and says, "I still need to find your brother and I can't trust you to take me."

"Why not?"

"Lots of reasons."

"Name three."

"One, you're bigger and stronger than me. If I untie you, you could simply walk away and there's little I could do about it."

"You've got a gun, remember?"

"Yeah, but we both know I'm not gonna shoot you."

"Excuse me, but didn't you just murder a man with your bare hands?"

She sighs. "If I shoot you I'll never find your brother. Reason number two, you could lead me on a wild goose chase. And three, you could be in on it with Jake, and if so, what's to stop you from leading me deep into the woods or bayous where you've got friends and family who'll see me coming from miles away? They'll overpower me and stick me in one of Jake's storage containers and force me to make fetish porn videos till I die from disease or exhaustion."

"That's crazy."

"Maybe so, but how can I know for certain?"

"Because I'm nothing like my brother."

"Interesting comment from a guy who said his brother would never kidnap my sister. Were you lying when you said that?"

"Is that what you *really* think happened? That Jake kidnapped Julie? He wouldn't *do* that. What's his *motive?*"

"Sex."

"Try again. Jake's got looks *and* money. He could get any woman he wants. And he *has.*"

"What do you mean?"

"He's been in a serious relationship for over a year."

Daisy's eyes go big. "With who?"

"His girlfriend. Not only that, but he's trying to *evade* the mob, so why would he bother to kidnap your sister?"

"She was his bookkeeper."

Bobby's expression changes. "Seriously?"

Daisy nods.

"Okay, so this is finally starting to make sense." He thinks about it a minute, then says, "According to you, this Zorba character didn't claim Jake *kidnapped* Julie, he only said Jake was involved in her disappearance. Maybe he helped her get away and she hasn't called you because she's laying low somewhere, without her phone. She probably dumped her phone so it couldn't be traced."

"That's encouraging to hear, but it doesn't get me any closer to finding Julie."

"What if I set up a meeting with Jake in a neutral place?"

"You could do that?"

"I can call and ask."

She stares at him a while before saying, "So you totally lied about the burner phone?"

"No. Jake definitely uses burners, and I don't know the numbers. But he also has a personal phone in his girlfriend's name."

She shakes her head. "You really *are* a conman."

"I'd rather you thought of me as a clever guy who was trying to save his life."

"You were quite convincing."

"Thank you."

"It wasn't a compliment." She pauses. "I really think you're wasting your time and talents on this Moon Pie scam."

"Why's that?"

"There are bigger opportunities out there."

"Like what?"

Chapter 11

"POLITICS. YOU'RE CERTAINLY qualified."

"In what way?"

"You're an unparalleled liar with zero remorse, low morals, and no empathy for others. You're dishonest, intellectually dull, and so lazy you haven't bothered to research even the most basic facts associated with your own con. You're vulgar, perverted, self-serving, and untrustworthy. You wanted to *seduce* me? Stop acting like the leader of the free world. Try being my friend."

"I think you're being terribly unfair."

"Tweet it to someone who gives a shit."

"Do you want to find your sister or not?"

"Of course. But I can't afford to walk into a trap."

He sighs. "Look, I'll admit that technically this John the Baptist thing's a scam, but surely you can see I'm helping people."

"Sorry, no. I can't see that at all."

"I'm only confirming what these people want to hear. I'm reinforcing their faith, giving them something to believe in."

"Call it what you want, but you're not doing it to help them. You're in it for the money."

"Of course! But if each party gets what they want from a transaction, they both benefit." He pauses. "Maybe you should take a good, hard look in the mirror before criticizing me."

"Why's that?"

"You're fucking a guy you don't like who murders people for a living. You're whoring yourself to get what you want."

"Do you honestly think fucking Vinny the Prick to find my sister is equivalent to charging gullible people to look at snack food?"

"I think it's worse. But at the very least, you're no better than me. And let's not forget you lied about being married, and about your dead husband's ring, and probably half a dozen other things, including breaking hospital rules and pretending to be a medical student."

"Fuck you, Bobby."

"Truth hurts, doesn't it?"

"Yeah, it does. But not as much as disappointment."

With great sarcasm, he says, "Well, I'm sorry I disappointed you."

"No, you're not. But you should be. And anyway, you're not the first."

They're quiet till Bobby says, "You claimed I have no empathy for others, but what about *you*? You're aware I'm still naked from the waist down, right? And tied up? Has it even crossed your mind the pain I'm in? That Eddie guy kicked the *shit* out of me! Can you really just stand there and not even offer to help me?"

"What are you proposing?"

"Untying me would be nice."

"Sorry, can't do that."

"Could you at least lift my chair to a sitting position and give me something for the pain?"

She walks behind him and attempts to lift his chair from the back, but he's too heavy, so she gets the longest rope Tony left after cutting her bindings, and ties it to the rope around Bobby's chest.

Then she loops the other end around the handle of his oven door and tries to use it like a pully, but the door pops open and breaks.

"Nice job!" he says.

"Fuck you, Bobby. It's not my fault you weigh twice as much as me."

"Just untie me, okay? I swear to God I won't hurt you."

"Maybe not, but you won't help me, either."

"Despite what you think, I'll gladly help you find your sister."

"*Gladly?*"

"I like you, Daisy. The long trip will give us a chance to get to know each other."

"Prove it. Give me Jake's phone number. I'll call, and put him on speaker. When he answers, you'll tell him two goons came to your trailer asking about him and Julie. You don't have to ask for details, just ask if she's alive. Do that, and I'll untie you."

"His number's on my cell phone."

"I sincerely doubt that, since Tony looked through your phone and computer records. Dumb as he was, I expect even *he* would have noticed if you had Jake's number on speed dial."

"Look under Eileen."

"Who's that, his girlfriend?"

"Yeah. If he's not at her place, she'll know how to find him."

"Where's her place?"

"Plaquemine."

"Is there, in fact, a fishing shack on that river no one can pronounce?"

"There is. And if Jake's hiding your sister, that's where she is. You wanna know the truth? She's probably not hiding at all. Jake probably stashed her in a hotel somewhere, and he's cheating on Eileen."

"My sister's not with him by choice, or she would've found a way to call me. You know what? Forget calling Jake. If he knows I'm looking for Julie we'll lose the element of surprise. I need to go to the fishing shack."

"It's a long drive."

"We've established that. Can I trust you to take me there?"

"What's it worth to you?"

"Everything."

"Normally I wouldn't take advantage of your situation, but I could sure use ten grand if you can spare it."

"I don't have any money."

"Ask your boyfriend."

"I ran away from him, remember?"

"Actually, no. You never mentioned that."

"Well, that's exactly what I did. When Joey Zorba made his dying confession and told me Jake had a brother, I told Vinny I was going to Nashville to help my mom with her pregnancy. When I got there, I looked you up on her computer, found out you worked at Sallee Hospital, drove there, found you, stuck my finger up your ass, and here we are."

"You must have *some* assets. You rented a luxury sedan."

"I have a credit card and a small amount of cash, but not ten grand. On the other hand, if that's what it takes to secure your cooperation, I can get it."

"When?"

"Within the hour."

Bobby studies her face. "I can't guarantee Julie's at the fishing shack, but I can take you there. Is that good enough?"

Daisy nods. "I also want to meet Eileen."

"Why?"

"If she knows about Julie, I'll be able to read it in her expression. In fact, I'd like to go to Eileen's house first."

Bobby says, "I'd feel better if you say we have a deal: you'll pay me ten grand to take you to Eileen's, and to Jake's cabin."

"And back."

"Of course."

"Deal."

She unties Bobby from the waist up, ties his wrists together in front of his body, then uses the boning knife to cut his legs and ankles free from the chair. When he's on his feet, she helps him get the rest of his clothes on, then loops a length of rope around his torso several times to keep his arms tucked close to his body.

"That's totally unnecessary," he says. "I already promised to help you."

"You did. But let's start the trip this way and see how it goes."

"Can you get me a pain pill?"

"Sure. Where do you keep them?"

"Medicine cabinet, back bathroom."

"I'd rather not walk past Tony. He's pretty gross, you know?"

"Please?"

She sighs. "Okay, but you owe me."

He rolls his eyes.

As she heads to his bedroom he calls out, "Can you bring the whole container? There should be about a dozen pills in it."

"Yeah, whatever."

Chapter 12

AFTER BOBBY SWALLOWS two Percocets, Daisy retrieves her ring and fake finger and puts them in her pocket. Then she wipes Eddie's saliva from the Moon Pie, puts it in a plastic Ziploc bag, and places it carefully in her purse. Then she locates a couple of plastic kitchen trash bags and a roll of paper towels and spends twenty minutes cleaning up the vomit, scrubbing the floor, washing surfaces, countertops, drawer handles, the knife, and anything else she might have touched. After washing out the two beer bottles, she removes the remaining beer from the fridge and pours the poisoned liquid down the sink, washes those bottles as well, and adds them to the trash bags, along with the ropes, and Tony's soiled clothes. Then she wets a paper towel and washes the dried blood from Bobby's face, puts his keys in her purse, looks around, and sighs.

"If I had time, I'd wash Tony and Eddie's clothes and dress them," Daisy says. "But I don't." She ties the trash bags tightly, then puts them in the trunk of her car.

When she re-enters the trailer, Bobby says, "What about the dead guys? We can't just *leave* them here! Their stench will ruin my trailer!"

"Sorry, but I can't get delayed by a police investigation. Vinny thinks I'm in Nashville visiting my pregnant mom, so time's working against us. I'm sorry about your trailer, but try to imagine what Rocco would do if he finds out we killed two of his men?"

"That's why we should dispose of the bodies."

"It's broad daylight. Someone would see us."

"Easy for you to say. You've got Vinny's protection. I've got...no one."

"That's not true."

"Oh yeah? Who have I got?"

"Me."

"Right. And I'm supposed to believe you'd help me?"

Daisy looks surprised. "Of course I would! How can you think otherwise?"

"You said some pretty harsh things about me."

"Yes I did, and every word was true: you're a hot mess, Bobby: an ex-con, a con artist, and a people poisoner. Even so, I never called you a whore."

He looks down at his feet. "Sorry about that."

Daisy moves closer and kisses his cheek. "But not once have I ever said you weren't worth saving."

"Does that mean I still have a chance with you?"

"Let's not get ahead of ourselves."

"Can we at least drag their bodies outside?"

"No. It's too risky, and they're too heavy for me to do it alone. And no, I'm not gonna untie you! At least not till we're on the road. But I'll turn your air conditioner up full blast to help preserve their bodies till we get back. Anything else you can think of?"

"Yeah. Don't forget to lock the door when we leave."

"Really Bobby?" She shakes her head. "You don't think that would make you the prime suspect if someone finds the bodies?"

"If the door's unlocked, someone's bound to come in."

"Good! Let *them* report the dead guys. We'll be out of town. It's a perfect alibi."

Bobby frowns. "I don't claim to be a forensics expert, but please correct me if I'm wrong: In your world, someone's gonna open the door, walk into my trailer, find two dead guys, and call the police."

"Exactly!"

"And when the cops show up they'll look at the scene and come to the conclusion these two wiseguys from Miami snuck into my trailer, turned the air conditioner up full blast, and simultaneously began vomiting for no apparent reason. Then they cleaned the trailer of all fingerprints, including their own, scrubbed the vomit from the floors and surfaces, while leaving it on their own clothes. Except for Tony, who has no clothes here at all."

"Stranger things have happened," Daisy says. "Believe me!"

"I'm trying to. So, after cleaning up everything but their clothes, Tony and Eddie inexplicably took Tony's clothes and the dirty paper towels somewhere off the premises, never to be found, only to drive *back* to my property, so Eddie could die on my kitchen floor, and Tony—who's been naked all this time—could experience the singular joy of climbing into my bed and shitting my sheets before dying. Is that your story?"

"Sounds good to me, and the shitty sheets are still there to prove it. Ready to go?"

Daisy opens the door and looks around. When she's convinced they aren't being observed, she leads him to her rental car and says, "Get in the front seat." When he does, she circles the car, climbs into the driver's seat, and fumbles around in her purse till she finds her keys. Then she starts the engine and notices a little girl approaching the car.

"*Shit!*"

Daisy lowers her window and forces a smile. "Hello there!"

The girl walks right up to the car, looks at Bobby's swollen face, and the ropes binding him, and giggles.

Daisy says, "What are *you* doing here? I thought the other trailers were empty."

"Not the third one. That's where me and Mama live."

"Where your mom right now?"

The little girl points to the woods.

Bobby says, "Those trees run a quarter mile. What businesses the town has are on the other side."

"What's your name?" Daisy says.

"Cindy."

"How old are you, Cindy?"

"Five."

"Your mom leaves you here alone all day?"

"No ma'am, just from one to six, when Bobby's here. He takes care of me sometimes."

Daisy turns and shows Bobby a look that suggests she might be seeing him in a different light. To Cindy, she says, "Can you keep a secret?"

Cindy stares through huge blue eyes and nods slowly.

"Don't tell anyone you saw Bobby tied up, okay?"

"You'll have to pay me."

"How much?"

"A million dollars."

"I'm fresh out of millions. How about five?"

"Okay."

Daisy pays her, and says, "Bobby and I are just playing a game with the ropes."

Cindy grins. "I know. He plays that same game with Mama, in her bedroom, when they think I'm sleeping."

Daisy clenches her teeth. "He does, huh?"

"Yes, ma'am."

"You know what, Cindy? Go ahead and tell your mom you saw Bobby playing that same game with me today."

"Okay!"

As Daisy backs the car onto the gravel road, Bobby says, "That was a shitty thing to do."

"Something tells me you'll be tying her mom back up in no time. There can't be much competition in this town."

"There's not. But I wouldn't have pegged you for the jealous type."

"Jealous?" Daisy laughs. "Keep dreaming, Gigolo. What are you looking at?"

"The empty space where a car should be."

"What are you talking about?"

"The car Tony and Eddie drove here. Where is it?"

"How would *I* know?"

"When I passed out, you didn't hear their tires on the gravel road?"

"If I had, Tony couldn't have snuck up behind me. I think they must have been hiding in your trailer before we got there."

"Which means someone must have dropped them off and could be watching us right now, from a distance."

"I don't think so. In my experience, crime goons travel in pairs. They probably parked on the other side of the trees." Daisy drives down the gravel road, turns right on 96.

Bobby says, "How'd you know which way to turn?"

"I didn't. I'm going back to the hospital."

"Why?"

"To get your ten grand."

"You left ten thousand bucks at the hospital this morning?"

"No, but *you* did!"

Chapter 13

WITH FOURTEEN STAFF members referred to as "chief" or "executive," Sallee Hospital is clearly more generous with titles than salaries. Greatly annoyed to see Horace Boudreaux, Executive Director of Operations standing in front of him, unannounced, Mark Michon, Chief Administrative Officer, hangs up his phone and says, "This better be important, Horace."

"There's a young lady in my office claiming sexual harassment."

Mark frowns. "When did *this* happen?"

"Around eleven this morning."

"That's bullshit!" He rubs his face and eyes. "Okay, what was said to her, who said it, and so forth?"

Horace grimaces. "She's claiming digital penetration."

"*What?* Jesus! Who's representing her?"

"She hasn't got an attorney."

"She *doesn't?*" Mark claps his hands together. "Well, ...that's *wonderful!* Thank God, and so forth. You need to get our guy over there, ASAP!"

"I've sent for him. But she wants a check right now, or she's going to take her story to the Times-Picayune."

"It's a shakedown."

"One hundred percent."

"Which means she's bluffing."

"I don't think so."

"Why not?"

"She's got thirteen witnesses."

"What the *fuck?*"

"We've already spoken to three of them, including Dr. Cormier and Bobby Cujo."

"Who's Cujo?"

"One of our part-time workers."

Michon stares out his window for fifteen seconds without speaking. And when he finally *does*, his words are clipped with anger and disbelief: "Are you trying to tell me our hospital and building security staff are so patently inept that thirteen people—including two of our employees—stood idly by while a young lady—one of our patients—got *finger*-fucked, and so forth? Who did it? Did he have a *gun?*"

"I've failed to make myself clear," Horace says, checking his watch. "Remember Robin Robicheau? The reporter who wrote the column that nearly put us out of business in 2008?"

"Robin the Bitch? Of *course*. What's *she* got to do with this?"

"She called Daisy's cell phone five minutes ago. I listened in, and it was definitely Robin's voice: after all these years it *still* sent chills down my spine. Anyway, Daisy told her to call back in twenty minutes for the story."

"Who the fuck is Daisy?"

"Daisy Pepper: the young lady in my office."

"The one who got *molested?*"

Boudreaux sighs. "She didn't get molested. She *perpetrated* the molesting."

Michon looks around. "This is a joke, right? You're fucking with me!"

"Look, we're running out of time, so let me summarize: this morning, Daisy Pepper ducked into our hospital to get away from a man she claims was stalking her. She followed staff members into our coed locker room, found some scrubs, put them on, and joined a group of eleven medical students under the direction of Dr. Milton Cormier. As they made their rounds, Daisy participated with the medical students in all activities including the digital rectal examination of our paid volunteer, Bobby Cujo."

"She's admitting she broke into our changing room, impersonated a medical student, and stuck her finger up Mr. Cujo's *ass*? I fail to see how that makes *us* liable! On the other hand, I'd say we have a *helluva* case against *her*!"

"Problem: she didn't break into the changing room. Dr. Cormier actually held the door open for her and told her to hurry. Apparently, he mistook her for a medical student."

"So, she's young enough to pass for a medical student, and Dr. Fuck-Me-In-The-Broom-Closet held the door for her. I'll take a wild guess she's attractive."

"More like gorgeous."

Michon frowns. "Cormier probably wanted to see what she looked like in her underwear. Did she claim he watched her get undressed, and so forth?"

"She did."

"How much did he see?"

"Bra and panties. She credits her easy access to poor hospital security. She also feels the *Times* would be fascinated to learn that doctors, nurses, and med students change clothes in the same locker room."

"That happens all over the country."

"Yes, but how many people *know* that? Daisy's confident that our doctors' wives will be furious when they read about it in the paper."

"She's right. But based on what you said, *she's* the one who committed sexual assault."

"That's correct."

"What's this Cujo character got to say about it?"

"He says he feels victimized. Claims he's a victim of sexual assault and it's the hospital's fault."

"So they're in it together."

"I can't be certain."

"Why not?"

"Someone beat him up."

"Did he say who?"

"No, and I didn't ask."

"Smart. The less we know the better off we'll be." Michon thinks a minute. "Robin the Bitch is calling her back for details?"

"Yes. And soon."

"Has Ms. Pepper revealed any part of this story to the *Times* yet?"

"No. And she's prepared to tell Robin the whole thing was a misunderstanding, and there *is* no story."

"Will she sign a full release, and so forth?"

"Yes."

"What about Cujo?"

"He'll sign a provisional one."

"What's that mean?"

"He wants to keep working here."

"He likes getting fingers up his ass?"

"Apparently."

"Well, that's not gonna happen. You threaten us, you can't get sodomized, that's my motto. In fact, I'm gonna put it on my stationary, first chance I get. What sort of name is Cujo, anyway? You ever hear that name before?"

"No, sir. But I think you should reconsider firing him."

"Why?"

"There's no one else."

"What're you talking about?"

"We pay him eleven dollars an hour for digital rectal exams. And that includes scrotal."

"You're shitting me!"

"No sir."

"You haven't said how much they're asking for. Let me guess: a million dollars, right? Everyone wants a million."

"Thirty thousand."

"What? Thirty grand each?"

"All together."

"Well...omigod, that's...*nothing*! What kind of shakedown artists *are* they? That's less than we'd pay to defend the case, hoping to settle for a hundred-fifty! Are you certain about this?"

"Quite."

"In that case, offer them five thousand, see what they say."

"I did. They refused."

"Did they counter?"

"Indeed. They're willing to accept ten thousand each if we can make a deal before Robin calls back."

"Here's what's bothering me: you know this number's dirt-cheap, and yet you didn't pay. Why?"

Boudreaux shrugs. "I'm not authorized to approve checks above five grand without board approval."

"I see. So, you came to me, to throw *my* ass in the fire!" He pauses. "Well, fine. Tell them we'll pay. But she'll have to convince Robin there's no story, and they'll both have to sign releases before getting their checks."

"How long will it take corporate to write the releases?"

"I don't know. We'll rush it. A day or two."

"Daisy and Bobby are willing to wait, but they want something to show good faith."

"Like what?"

"A down-payment. In cash."

"How much?"

"Five hundred."

Michon digs through his pockets, removes a money clip, counts out $280. "How much do *you* have?"

"Two hundred."

Michon hands his cash to Boudreaux, borrows twenty bucks from his secretary, and tells him to hurry and make the deal. Then he asks his secretary, "Who's our head of security?"

"Doug Blaine."

"Call Mr. Blaine and tell him I need to speak with him immediately. Then see if you can locate the architectural firm that designed the hospital. Tell them I need a copy of the blueprints, and so forth. There's got to be a room in this God-forsaken hospital we can turn into a separate changing space before the *Times* sends a reporter to snoop around. I swear, this Daisy Pepper bitch is something else: she saved us a fortune in bad publicity while robbing us of twenty grand, using nothing more than her index finger as a weapon."

Chapter 14

"YOU'RE NOT GONNA tie me up again?" Bobby says.

"What's the point? I'm not brave enough to shoot you, strong enough to overpower you, or fast enough to chase you. Plus, you could have got away anytime you wanted in the hospital just now, and didn't. And anyway, it's to your advantage to stay with me till we get our settlement from the hospital."

"Those are all good points, but you left out the most important one: I *like* you. A lot!"

"No you don't, you just think I'm hot. The one you *like* is Cindy's mom, from the trailer park."

"You can't be serious! *Stacy?* I mean, have you *seen* her? She's a booty call, nothing more. You, on the other hand, ...you're..."

Daisy looks at him, waits to hear what she is. Oddly, he can't seem to settle on a word, so she offers: "Classy? Perfect? A princess? A goddess? Wife material?"

"I was gonna say you're different."

"Why didn't you?"

"I didn't think it would sound strong enough."

"You were right."

Bobby frowns. "Any chance we can stop somewhere and have a drink before hitting the road?"

"Why?"

"Eddie hit me pretty hard, but the floor hit harder. I think I might have a concussion."

"You think it's wise to drink with a concussion?"

"Not even. But it'll make me feel better."

Daisy says, "Are you aware that concussions are traumatic brain injuries and alcohol's a neurotoxin?"

"Actually, my medical knowledge is limited to rectums and scrotums."

"Well, it's true: alcohol kills brain cells. It's also a depressant that could impede your recovery while elevating your risk factors."

"Risk factors for what?"

"Depression."

Bobby laughs. "Have you ever seen a more depressing existence than mine?"

"Yes."

"Not counting those who are sick, injured, broke, or addicted."

"Then, no. Yours is the most depressing."

"It's just a few drinks, Daisy. We don't have to get plastered, or anything. And anyway, you're driving."

"What's your drink of choice?"

"Beer."

"You can have two. No more. Why are you grinning?"

"It's been a long time since I let a woman tell me what to do."

"It shows. Stop grinning. You look like that comedian who laughs at his own jokes."

"Adam Sandler?"

"The other one."

"Jerry Seinfeld?"

"No. The big guy."

"Vince Vaughn?"

"Yeah."

Bobby's grin morphs into a smile.

"*Now* what?" Daisy says.

"You don't want to admit it, but you like me."

"I'm using you."

"Maybe so, but I can tell when someone likes me."

"What's the closest bar?"

"Zeegar's."

"Point the way."

Bobby does, and when they get there, it's full, but there's a restaurant side, so they claim a four-top, sit down, and within seconds, two waiters show up.

"Hi," one says. "I'm Darryl, and I'll be your waiter this evening." He hands them menus and says, "This is Ambrose. He's in training."

Bobby says, "There's gotta be twenty waiters in here, and only a dozen tables. Why's that?"

The waiters look at each other. Darryl says, "There's a lot of turnover. Can I get you folks a cocktail?"

"Beer for me," Bobby says.

Darryl looks at Daisy.

"Iced tea," she says.

"Sweetened, or unsweetened?"

"You're joking, right?"

Her comment seems to throw Darryl. He and Ambrose look at each other.

"Surprise me," Daisy says.

They leave, and Bobby says, "How come Vinny the Prick hasn't called you?"

"What makes you think he hasn't?"

"I haven't heard your phone ring."

She digs into her handbag for her phone and shows it to him. "This is the ancient phone I left at my mom's house last time I went there. Only three people on earth have the number, and Vinny's not one of them. You want to be the fourth?"

"Of course! Thank you!"

"My pleasure."

After exchanging numbers, he asks, "Who are the other three?"

"Alma, Sophie, and Julie."

"Julie's your sister. Who are the other two?"

"Alma's my mom, and Sophie's my old girlfriend from high school." She looks around. "I need to pee. Can I count on you not to run away before I get back?"

"Of course."

When Daisy stands to leave she nearly bumps into two young men carrying her and Bobby's drinks. "I'm Robby," one says, "And this is Alex. Have you guys had a chance to look over your menus yet?"

"We're not dining tonight," Daisy says. "What happened to Darryl and Ambrose?"

"Who?"

"The guys that took our drink order two minutes ago."

"Oh. They no longer work here."

"Did something happen?"

"What do you mean?"

Bobby says, "I'll order my second beer now, and take my chances on who's gonna bring it."

Daisy heads to the restroom and takes her time returning. By then, Bobby's half-way through his second beer.

"In case you're interested," he says, "Robby and Alex still work here. Why are you staring at me like that?"

"I'm trying to decide how tough you are."

"Why?"

"I need to know if you can protect me."

"In that case, fear not: I'm tough enough."

"Even with a possible concussion and bruised ribs?"

"Even with. Don't worry, Daisy, I won't let anyone hurt you. You have my word."

"Thank you, Bobby."

She glances at the bar, holds her hand high over her head, and makes a gesture like she's summoning someone. Seconds later a massive shadow covers their table. Bobby looks up and sees a hulking beast of a man towering over them. Daisy says, "Gerald, this is Bobby. Bobby? Meet Gerald."

Bobby appraises him. "How long have you two known each other?"

"About two minutes," Daisy says. "We met in the bar."

"And he's standing here because?"

"I asked the bartender who the toughest guy in the bar was, and he said Gerald, by far."

"You hired him to protect us?"

"Not exactly."

"Then why's he here?"

"I told Gerald if he can beat your ass, I'd give him a blow job."

Bobby's eyes go wide as he takes in Gerald's grin.

Bobby says, "What am I missing? Weren't we just talking about my bruised ribs and possible concussion?"

"Yes, of course. That's why I only asked for one guy instead of three."

Gerald narrows his eyes. "You ready to do this?"

"Can I finish my beer first?"

"No."

Bobby looks at Daisy. "This guy's twice my size."

"No, he's not."

Bobby studies Gerald with a critical eye. "I'm pretty sure he is."

"Even so, it should be easier than fighting three men at the same time."

Bobby nods. "You might be right, depending on the guys. Can I at least take a piss first?"

She looks at Gerald and says, "That seems fair."

Gerald thinks it over. "Awright. But make it quick."

As Bobby heads to the restroom, Gerald says, "I like blow jobs." Then he says, "Aw, Shit!"

"What's wrong?"

Gerald rushes across the room, out the front door, and leaves her sitting there.

Chapter 15

NOW, IN THE parking lot, Bobby's grinning like Kim Kardashian's esthetician after a butt wax. "Hey, Daisy! Ready to go to Eileen's?"

"I am," she says. "But we should probably swing by the hospital first."

"Why?"

"Just to check things out, make sure you're okay."

"Maybe we should take Gerald!" Bobby says, laughing.

She'd respond, but Bobby just passed out in the middle of his laugh. When he comes to he says, "Where am I?"

"Parking lot, Zeegar's."

"What happened?"

"What's the last thing you remember?"

"I went to take a piss."

"Right. Okay, so you went to the men's room, took your shoe off, broke the window, climbed out, and tried to escape. And you would have, but Gerald was behind the building waiting for you."

"Then what happened?"

"He beat the piss out of you, and here you are. I must say, I'm disappointed in you, Bobby."

"Oh yeah? Well, I'm disappointed in *you*, too!"

"How are your hands?" she says.

"My hands?"

"Yeah."

Bobby wiggles his fingers. "Fine, far as I can tell. Why do you ask?"

"I was being facetious. You didn't land a single punch."

"Fuck you!"

Daisy sighs. "Let's see if you can stand."

It takes him a minute, but with the help of a couple of bystanders, Bobby gets to his feet, wincing. He staggers a couple of times before gaining his footing. "Did you blow him out here in front of everyone?"

"Don't be ridiculous."

"Thank God!"

"I blew him in the men's room."

"*What?*"

Daisy laughs. "I'm joking. *Jesus*, Bobby: is that how you really see me?"

"Gerald let it slide?"

"Yeah."

"He doesn't seem the type."

"It took some doing, but I convinced him."

"How?"

"I've got a gun, remember?"

"You threatened to shoot him?"

"Not exactly. Yes, I held my gun on him, but I also offered him $500. And he took it."

"You gave him all our money?"

"Just our hospital advance. I've still got some cash and a credit card. Ready to go to the hospital? They're paying."

"No way! Those bastards will keep us there all night and jack the price of treatment so high we won't get half our settlement. Just take me to the BHS."

"What's that?"

"Twenty-four-hour clinic, basic Doc-in-the-box. There's one close by, on Mansfield Road. They can stitch me up and get us back on the road in no time."

"Sounds like a plan."

Chapter 16

TO DISTRACT BOBBY while the doctor stitches his face, Daisy says, "Tell me about Jake."

"What about him?"

"Just the stuff I'd want to know: how old is he, has he ever been married, where'd he go to school, how much money he has...."

"Jake's the golden boy. He's 34, never been married."

"Far as you know."

"I'd know."

"You said you guys aren't close. He and Eileen *could've* gotten married secretly."

"Not possible. As for your other questions, everyone in the parish knew Jake Cujo's name. He was a legendary athlete: football, basketball, track...and smart, too: when he got hurt, Tulane pulled his athletic scholarship, but it didn't slow him down. He applied for—and got—an academic scholarship, and graduated *summa cum laude.*"

"So, Jake got the brains, you got the *looks?*"

Bobby laughs. "Not even close. Like I said, he's the golden boy. He got it all. He got the millions, I got the Moon Pies."

"How'd he wind up in the storage business?"

He cocks his head at her and says, "Why do I get the impression you know more about Jake than you're letting on?"

"Because it's true. But I don't know much about *college* Jake."

Bobby nods. "Okay, so he was in graduate school, getting his master's in engineering. Took a job as a cost analyst at a shipping yard. Came up with an idea for a new type of shipping container, but kept it to himself. After graduating, he made it happen: some sort of polymer he molded around a steel shell that cut the weight 60% while maintaining 90% of the structural integrity. Suddenly, ships could carry the same cargo with less weight, saving millions each year in fuel costs. He got some financial backing, and made millions."

"What caused the rift between you?"

"I'd rather not talk about that."

After leaving the doctor's office, they get in Daisy's car. She turns on the engine, checks the fuel gauge. "Where's the nearest truck stop?"

"Take a right out of the parking lot and keep going. It's about three miles, on the right side of the road. You can't miss it."

Daisy backs out of her parking space, exits the parking lot, guides the car onto the main road. "If you haven't spoken to Jake in a year, how'd you know he was hiding from the mob?"

"Eileen told me. She said a hitman killed his partner Sully, and Jake went off the grid and I'd better erase all his information from my phone, computer, and social media accounts, or take the risk of being targeted."

"Did she tell you why the mob got involved in his business?"

"No. Do *you* know?"

"Yes. But I doubt you'll believe me."

"I'm willing to listen."

"Jake's containers were cooler in the summer, warmer in the winter than the old steel ones, so they became the preferred method for traffickers to ship live humans. Organized crime wanted in on the action, but Jake and Sully refused, so they killed Sully and made Jake an offer he couldn't refuse."

"The mob wouldn't go to that much trouble for human trafficking."

"True, but that's what got their attention. Except that they wanted Jake to pour a four-inch layer of plastic into the bottom of the containers to cover small carbon-fiber boxes filled with diamonds. That's how they paid the cartels for product."

"Which product?"

"Heroin. The cartels would receive the containers, chip off the plastic, replace the diamonds with heroin, cover the heroin with a layer of plastic, and ship them back. But they needed Jake to give the polymer formula to the cartels so they could pour it from their end. With a gun to his head, Jake agreed, but he gave them a bogus formula, which bought him enough time to skim millions from the business. Then he went into hiding."

Bobby frowns. "How did they find out I was his brother?"

"There aren't many Cujo's floating around. They probably did an online search and found the notice of your mother's death that listed you and Jake as survivors."

"At least the goons in my trailer didn't know about Eileen."

"I'm sure he kept their relationship a secret."

"But now *you* know..."

"So?"

"If you decide to tell *Vinny*, all three of us are screwed: me, Jake, *and* Eileen."

"I wouldn't do that."

"I hope not. But I took a huge chance telling you about Eileen. And you've told me virtually nothing about yourself."

"What's your point?"

"I feel you have an obligation to tell me something about yourself that no one knows."

"Why?"

"Because thanks to you, there are two dead guys in my trailer, and I got the shit beat out of me twice, and the information I just gave you about Jake could get me killed."

"Your logic is faulty, Robert. First of all, the guys in the trailer had nothing to do with me. They were looking for Jake and would have been there whether you met me or not. Secondly, while you most certainly got your ass beat twice, only the second time was my fault. But only partly, because you assured me you could protect me. And by the way, I wasn't trying to get you hurt, I was trying to gather information about your fighting skills so I'll be able to make intelligent decisions when our lives are on the line. As for giving me information that could get you killed? Tony would have gotten that from you within minutes. On the other hand, if not for me, you never would have gotten untied, and you wouldn't be collecting $10,000 from the hospital."

"Minus the $500 you gave Gerald."

"I'll deduct the $500 from my part of the settlement, and that should make us more than even."

"I'd agree if you'd been remotely honest with me. My problem is, I don't believe half the things you've said."

"Like what?"

"I don't believe you studied blue coral snakes in Bangkok. I don't believe you started fucking Vinny because he agreed to find your sister. I don't believe Joey Zorba got stabbed with an ice pick and made the dying confession that my brother had something to do with Julie's disappearance."

"I see. Well, for your information, I never said I studied blue coral snakes in Bangkok. I said blue corals were indigenous to that area."

Bobby considers it, and says, "Okay, that one's on me. What about the rest?"

"Is that the truck stop?"

"It is. If you turn in and pull up to a pump and use your credit card, I'll pump the gas."

She does, and he does, and when he climbs back in the car she says, "Who were you talking to on your phone just now?"

"Stacy."

"Booty call Stacy?"

"Yeah."

"What's on *her* mind?"

"Cindy found the dead guys in the trailer."

"Did they call the cops?"

"She says no, but if she's lying, we're screwed."

"Why's that?"

"I told her where we are."

Daisy groans. "*Why?*"

He shrugs. "She asked. It took me by surprise. I answered without thinking."

"Did you tell her you were with *me*?"

"Yeah, and she's not happy about it. But I doubt she'll tell the cops, 'cause they'd probably put Cindy in child services. Can we get some water and snacks for the road?"

"Yeah. And I need to pee."

"I thought you peed at Zeegar's."

"I would have, but Gerald was anxious to meet you."

Bobby frowns, thinking about it. "Sorry I disappointed you. But that wasn't a fair fight."

Daisy says, "I wasn't disappointed you lost, Bobby. I was disappointed you tried to run away."

Noticing the main building of the truck stop has both a diner and convenience store, Daisy drives to the front entrance, parks, and they go inside without saying another word.

Chapter 17

NOW, IN THE convenience store, Bobby grabs four bottles of water from the refrigerated case, cradles them in the nook of his left arm, and stands in the checkout line behind six guys. Daisy finds him, places her credit card and several bags of snacks on top of the waters he's holding, which forces Bobby to use both hands to keep everything balanced. From a distance, you'd think he's holding a baby, and the image isn't lost on Daisy, who laughs, spins around, and heads to the bathroom, with every man's eyes firmly fixed on her rear end, including Bobby's. When it's his turn to check out, he stacks his purchases on the counter, slides Daisy's credit card through the reader, picks up the plastic stylus and signs his name. When the cashier bags his groceries, he walks to the front door and waits for Daisy to join him.

More than five minutes pass before she exits the ladies' room and when she does, she breezes past him in a huff and goes straight to the car. Annoyed, Bobby follows her and climbs into the passenger seat. Daisy starts the engine and says, "Direct me, please."

Bobby punches *Plaquemine* into her navigation screen, then holds up her credit card and asks, "Who's Leah Shea?"

Daisy sighs. "I don't know. Probably some poor dead woman. Or possibly the recent victim of identity theft. It's the card Vinny gave me last week so I could buy something nice after he cheated on me."

"Did he tell you what the limit was?"

"He said to keep the charges under three grand."

"Good to know, but I was talking about how long before it might be reported as stolen."

"He wouldn't give me a card with a time limit."

Daisy puts the car in reverse, and the computer voice barks out a command. Bobby lowers the volume and says, "Why do you care if Vinny cheated on you?"

"I don't. And anyway, he's married, so it's a moot point. But apparently, it matters to Vinny."

"What did he give his wife for this latest indiscretion?"

"I haven't a clue. Nor do I care."

As she backs out of the parking space, Bobby says, "You think he rewards *her* every time he has sex with *you*?"

"No." Then, in a clipped voice, she adds: "I think he feels entitled to one mistress. Have we reached the limit on rude, inappropriate questions you wanted to ask?"

"Not remotely. But I'll save the others till we're in bed together."

"Yeah, well that's not gonna happen."

"Sorry, but it's inevitable." He pauses. "Are you feeling okay?"

"Why are you asking?"

"You were in the bathroom a long time."

"Believe it or not, I ran into someone I knew."

He looks at her. "Seriously?"

Daisy navigates the car through the truck stop parking lot, turns right on the highway and says, "Vinny hired a private investigator named Dani Ripper to locate me, and she did. She confronted me in the restroom just now."

"*Fuck!*"

"It's okay. He took her off the case."

"Why?"

"He only hired her to make sure I was okay."

"You spoke to Vinny?"

"No."

"Who'd you say Vinny hired?"

"Dani Ripper."

"Why does that name sound familiar?"

"You remember the Little Girl Who Got Away? Mindy Renee Whittaker?"

"I think so. What about her?"

"Same person, different name. She grew up and became a private investigator."

"Did she tell Vinny we're together?"

"Yes. But she told him you didn't appear to be a threat since you'd been mugged."

"You said you *know* her? How, from TV?"

Daisy ignores the question. "Tell me about Jake's girlfriend, Eileen."

"What do you want to know?"

"Do you like her?"

"I'm not a huge fan."

"Why not?"

Bobby sighs. "Do we really need to get into this?"

"We do."

"She's my wife."

Chapter 18

DAISY NEARLY RUNS off the road. "Your *wife?* You're *married?*"

"Technically, yes."

"Jake ran off with your *wife?*"

"She ran off with him."

"What's the difference?"

"She pursued him. He allowed it to happen, but she's the one who forced it."

"Were you and Jake close before that happened?"

"I thought so. Then again, he never offered me any opportunities with his company, so..."

"How long were you married before she bailed?"

"A year."

"Was it all about the money? The lifestyle?"

"Sadly, no. It was all about Jake. Like all the others, she wanted him from the day they met. He could have been broke, it wouldn't have mattered."

"But the millions didn't hurt."

"I suppose not."

Daisy takes her eyes off the road to look at him. "She hurt you."

"Yup."

"What a *bitch!*"

They ride in silence for twenty minutes. "When's the last time you saw her?"

"The day she left."

"No *shit?* But you've *spoken* to her, right?"

"Just that time she told me Jake was in hiding."

"Well, *this* should be interesting."

He laughs.

Daisy says, "If I ask you something will you promise to be honest?"

"Of course."

"Don't just say what you think I want to hear."

"I understand what honest means. What's your question?"

"Is she prettier than me?"

"No."

"Close?"

He thinks a moment. "I'd rate you a ten."

"And Eileen?"

"A nine."

"You're sure?"

"Positive. Does that make you happy?"

"Relieved. I'd hate to meet two women prettier than me on the same night."

"Who's the other one?"

"Dani Ripper."

"I sincerely doubt she's in your league."

"I'm not fishing for compliments. I know most guys consider me hot, but she's one-of-a-kind."

"Well, I wouldn't give you up for her, no matter what she looks like."

Surprisingly, Daisy snaps: "I'm not yours to *give*, Robert."

"Well, fuck you, too!" he says, and immediately regrets it. Still wounded, he says, "That was meant as a compliment."

"I know. I'm sorry."

"You called me Robert."

"So?"

"I don't like that."

She winks. "I know."

A minute passes. "What's Daisy short for?"

"Nothing. It's my full name."

"What's your middle name?"

"I'm not telling. This way I can *Robert* you whenever I feel like it, and there's nothing you can say back."

"You're a pistol, you are."

"Remember that."

A half hour later Daisy shakes him. "Are you okay?"

"Huh?"

"There's no danger going to sleep after suffering a concussion, provided your pupils aren't dilated, and you can walk okay and carry on a conversation. But you slurred your words and drifted off. I called your name, but you weren't responsive."

"Oh. Thanks. I'm okay. Just sleeping."

"You don't snore?"

"Not that I know of."

"Well, *that's* a plus. How's your pain?"

"I'm okay. I took another Percocet at the truck stop." He checks the navigation screen. "We're getting close. Want to go straight to Eileen's?"

"No. I want to check into a hotel and get cleaned up before I meet your wife."

"She'll be asleep by then."

"We'll wake her."

"She'll call the cops."

"No, she won't. She'll want to see who you're dating."

"Are we talking about you?"

"Yup. She'll want to check me out."

"Why?"

"It's what we do."

"You're gonna pretend to be my girlfriend?"

"I can play that part if you like. You said I'm prettier. We could tweak her a bit."

"I'd like that. Thank you."

"Just don't get too handsy, trying to impress her."

"Okay, but Daisy?"

"Yeah?"

"I really do like you."

"I know."

"That's all you've got to say?"

"Try to remember, I've known you exactly one day."

"In dog years, maybe. But in people time we've spent every minute together for the past twelve hours. That's like *four* dates for most people, not to mention all the stress we've been through."

"Nice speech. But I'm not sleeping with you on our first day."

"I know. But what about our first night?"

She glances at his face, illuminated by the interior lighting. "I admire your persistence. I know you're in a lot of pain and you're still trying to get in my pants. I'm flattered."

"Like I said, I really like you. And I'm on drugs, so the pain isn't that bad."

"It will be, soon enough. Your face looks like it's been run through a thresher. I should have insisted on a plastic surgeon. And x-rays of your ribs. They're bound to be seriously bruised or cracked. You pissed at the doctor's office, didn't you?"

"Yeah."

"Did you see any blood?"

"No."

"Are you just saying that because you want to sleep with me?"

"Yes. But seriously, I'm fine. Sure, I'm banged up, but it's not gonna affect my performance."

Daisy laughs. "*Performance?* Does that mean you expect applause afterward?"

"Only if it's genuine. What's a thresher?"

"A farm machine that grabs plants and beats them till their seeds fall out."

Bobby says, "You can thresh *me*, if you want."

"Maybe I'll just watch while you thresh yourself. Will that work?"

"It's a start."

Chapter 19

IT'S CLOSING IN on ten p.m. when they get to Plaquemine. After doing a quick drive-by of Eileen's house, they check into a nearby hotel—one room, two beds—and Bobby says, "Maybe we should wait till tomorrow." His speech is groggy.

Daisy asks if Eileen has a job.

"Probably. She used to be the top realtor in the parish."

"Commercial or residential?"

"Residential."

"Did she follow a schedule?"

She used to wake up early, got her paperwork done by nine, made calls, then spent the rest of the day showing houses or visiting properties."

"What you're saying, if she's still working real estate, we'll be able to catch her at home tomorrow morning."

"Exactly."

"Good to know. But at the rate your face is swelling I doubt she'll be able to recognize you by then."

"If you really want to go tonight, I'm up for it."

She appraises his face: cut, swollen, bruised, bandaged...and the bandages black from the blood that leaked from his stitches, post-suture. His clothes are the same ones he wore this morning, but unlike her, it's the only outfit he has for the entire trip. His shirt and pants are ripped and caked with dried blood, dirt, and assorted filth acquired from his encounter with Gerald at Zeegar's. If she were Bobby she wouldn't let a total stranger see her in this condition, let alone his runaway wife. But since he'll only look worse tomorrow, she decides to make the visit tonight, soon as she takes a shower and puts on some lipstick and eyeliner. She tells him to take another pain pill and lie down and get some rest while she showers.

As expected, by the time she exits the bathroom, Bobby's completely zonked. She removes the spread from her bed and drapes it over him. Then grabs her handbag, checks to make sure she has her phone, car and room keys, then quietly closes the door and drives to Eileen's house, and arrives just in time to see her being escorted into an ambulance.

Chapter 20

THE AMBULANCE LIGHTS are flashing, but there's no siren, and it's traveling at normal speed. Daisy follows it to the hospital, which turns out to be a couple of blocks from the hotel where she and Bobby are staying. She stops a short distance behind the ambulance and watches as the driver gets out, opens the back door, and helps the attendant get Eileen down the step. First thing Daisy notices, Eileen's as attractive as advertised: maybe not a *strong* nine, but a solid one, and classy, with an imperious sophistication that's evident even now, in her time of need, whatever her medical issue might be.

Though the attendant is guiding her, Eileen's walking without help and doesn't appear to be bleeding, hurt, or in serious pain. Daisy watches them disappear into the emergency room, then drives back to the hotel, enters the room, nudges Bobby. "Wake up!"

"Huh?"

"Get up! We've got work to do!"

It takes him a few minutes to get in motion, and she uses the time to explain how she followed Eileen's ambulance to the hospital.

"What's wrong with her?"

"I don't know. But like I said, it doesn't appear to be serious."

"Should we check on her?"

"Absolutely! First thing tomorrow. But right now we've got a window of opportunity and we need to seize it."

"What do you mean?"

"Her house is empty."

"So?"

"There'll never be a better time to search it!"

While Bobby spends a few minutes in the bathroom, Daisy changes into casual clothes and removes her scant makeup with a couple of moist wipes and a tissue. On the way to Eileen's house she says, "Have you ever broken into someone's house?"

"In the old days? Sure."

"What's the best way? Bust a window and reach inside, open the lock?"

"Probably. But we may not have to do that tonight since Eileen has a lock on her back door that uses a code that she never changes."

"Why won't she change it?"

"She's too lazy to read the manual."

"That can't be true."

"Believe it. She grew up a debutante, oblivious to crime. She lives in a bubble of trust. It would never dawn on her that someone might figure out her house code, even though she uses the same four digits for everything: her phone, computer, room safes at hotels..."

"If she's been dating Jake all this time I bet he reprogrammed it."

"Maybe. But that would require her learning a new code, and I'm guessing she resisted. We'll know soon enough."

They park the car a safe distance away and stroll casually down the sidewalk till they get to Eileen's house. Then Daisy climbs the steps to the porch and rings the doorbell while Bobby makes his way toward the back of the house. A minute later, the interior lights come on and he greets her at the front door sporting a wide grin. "Do you love me *now?*"

"No, but your stock is definitely rising!"

As she enters the foyer Bobby says, "I shouldn't have told you about the code. I missed my chance to impress you with my breaking and entering skills."

"It wouldn't have mattered. I already factored your jail time into the equation. Did you say she uses the same code for her computer?"

He nods.

"What is it?"

He tells her.

"I don't suppose you happen to know her email password?"

Bobby grins. "Possibly."

"I'll need it."

"What's it worth to you?"

"I've already offered ten grand."

"That was to bring you here. This goes *way* beyond that."

Daisy glances around the room. "How many bedrooms are there?"

"Three."

"And how do you know so much about this house?"

"It's her childhood home. Her parents gave it to her when they moved to Florida. I did all the renovations when we were dating. Can I ask *you* something? Why do you care how many bedrooms she has?"

"I want to know which bed she uses to fuck Jake."

"That would be the king bed in her room."

"You're positive?"

"One hundred percent."

"What makes you so sure?"

"She's weird about stuff like that. When her parents left, she made me move their bed, furniture, and wall hangings to the upstairs guest room, which is where they sleep when they come to visit. She would never have sex in her parents' bed."

"What about the other bedroom?"

"That's where she slept as a kid. Again, she wouldn't have sex there. And by the way, when her parents moved out, she wouldn't even *sleep* in the master bedroom till I put in new carpet, painted the walls, ceiling, and bathroom cabinets; installed a new toilet, new sinks...then she bought a new bed, new sheets, spread, pillows, and pillow cases. I literally had to remove every semblance of her parents from the master bedroom before she'd let me spend the night with her."

"I'd like to see your handiwork. Will you show me?"

He leads her down the hall, into Eileen's bedroom, and turns on the light.

Daisy glances around. "Is it exactly the way you left it? Same paint? Same bedspread?"

Bobby nods.

They walk into the master bathroom. "Is that the toilet you installed? And the sinks?"

"Yes."

"Nice job."

"Thanks."

She opens a drawer, frowns, then opens another. Then checks the medicine cabinet, and another drawer, then enters the shower and checks the shampoo bottles on the ledge. Finally, she says, "I'm confused: where's Jake's stuff?"

Bobby suddenly comes to life. He searches the cabinet under the sink.

Nothing.

Daisy says, "Check her closet, especially the dirty clothes hamper, if she's got one."

He does, and says, "No sign of Jake. Maybe she makes him keep his shit upstairs. What are you looking at?"

"The ceiling. "Is that your work?"

He nods.

Daisy makes a sweeping gesture with her arm and says, "So, you did all this work...how many hours did it take?"

"I don't know. Hundreds."

"So, after doing all this work, your lovely princess finally allowed you to fuck her in this very bed."

"That's correct."

"And a year or so later, Jake waltzes into her life, and Eileen—without requiring him to lift so much as a finger, or make a single change to the room or furnishings—fucked him every night in that same bed."

Bobby gives her a look. "Do you enjoy rubbing this in my face?"

"Of course not."

"Well, that's unfortunate, because you just succeeded in planting that image firmly in my mind: the one where my brother—and boyhood hero—fucks my wife in the same room where I labored hundreds of hours trying to make her happy. Thank you so much. I might have gone my whole life without making that connection."

"Relax, Bobby. I was only asking because I wanted to make certain this is the exact bed where Jake gives it to her every night he's in town."

"Then, by all means, be happy in the knowledge. This is the bed. Can I ask why it's so goddamn important to you?"

"Yes. It's because your wife's a world-class bitch and I can't think of any sweeter revenge you could have than to fuck me in her bed after I get the information I need from her computer."

He does a double take. "Seriously?"

Daisy nods.

"*Tonight?*"

She nods again.

"In that case, follow me."

Chapter 21

HE LEADS HER to the kitchen, where Eileen keeps her laptop on the built-in desk. Bobby opens it, moves the mouse till the screen lights up, then proudly points to the desktop folder titled: *Passwords*.

Daisy grimaces at Eileen's stupidity, opens the folder, and scrolls to the entry marked: *Gmail Account*. She notes Eileen's user name and password, then goes online and types it in. As the screen pops up, Bobby says, "Is there anything you need me to do?"

"If you're being serious, then yes."

"Name it."

"This is a request, not an order."

"Okay."

"Would you consider conducting a full-scale search of the house and garage?"

"Define full-scale."

"I'd like you to check every drawer and possible hiding place you can think of, paying special attention to her underwear drawer and the console, glove compartment, and trunk of her car. And her mail pile."

"No problem. What am I looking for?"

"Cell phones, and anything that can tell us where Jake might be, aside from his fishing shack."

"*Then* what?"

"Search the upstairs closets. If you find his clothes, pick out something nice, but don't put it on till after you've taken a shower. By then, I should be finished."

"Sounds great."

Twenty minutes later, Bobby returns. "Got a sec?"

She looks up from the computer screen.

He says, "No cell phones, nothing in her mail, nothing in her car, no clothes in the closets or bedrooms. I'm telling you all this, but you don't seem surprised. How come?"

"They broke up."

"Her and Jake? How do you know?"

"Any emails they may have shared have been deleted."

"That doesn't mean anything. He's on the run, and they're being careful. I wouldn't expect them to correspond by text or email. They probably communicate with burner phones exclusively."

"And yet you haven't found any."

"She probably took it to the hospital."

"I'm not saying it's impossible, but here's the thing: she's been dating someone else."

"*What? Who?*"

"Guy named David Cage. Ever heard of him?"

Bobby shakes his head. "It's gotta be a smokescreen. She's probably seeing this guy to throw the mob off her trail. Meanwhile, she's staying in contact with Jake."

Daisy says, "She and Cage have exchanged hundreds of emails. Their romance is all over Facebook. There's talk of an engagement."

"Then why aren't *his* clothes in the house?"

"The guy's a multi-millionaire. She stays at his place. At least she *used* to, till the incident."

"What do you mean?"

"I know why Eileen's in the hospital."

He looks at her.

"Brace yourself."

"Stop being so dramatic."

"Eileen has an ant colony in her head."

"Excuse me?"

"There are hundreds of ants living in her head. Every day dozens escape through her ears, but the ones inside her head keep reproducing at a rate that exceeds the turnover."

"That's ridiculous!"

"According to her emails, doctors have tried everything short of surgery: eardrops, heat...they even flushed her ears with an antiseptic solution to *drown* them. The reason she's in the hospital, they're gonna use laparoscopic cameras to see if they can locate and kill the queen. If that doesn't work, they're considering surgery that—even if it works—will render her deaf in one ear."

"Is it painful?"

"Most of the time, apparently not. But when it *does* hurt it's so bad that her doctors fear they might be chewing a path to her brain. Still wanna fuck me in her bed?"

"Of course!"

She shows him a look of surprise, then says, "I'll want to turn the spread down first."

"Makes sense to me."

They go to Eileen's bedroom and turn on the lights. Bobby pulls back the bedspread and...

Chapter 22

THE BED'S INFESTED with ants! A hundred, possibly more, are crawling all over her sheets and pillowcases.

"That's it," Daisy says. "I'm out of here."

Moments later, standing in front of the car, shuddering, slapping herself wherever her hands can reach, Bobby says, "Do you *ever* deliver on your sex promises?"

"Don't start with me," she says. Then looks at him incredulously. "You're *joking*, right?"

"Not at all. Do you realize in the space of one day you've reneged on sex promises three times?"

"Not true."

"Oh, really? You promised Tony from Miami a blow job, and killed him instead. Then you promised Gerald a blow job for kicking my ass, and paid him off instead. And now this."

"I'm sorry," Daisy says. "What's the third one?"

"Me. Just now."

"For your information, I never said we weren't gonna do it. I'm just not gonna do it in that house. If you're not willing to have sex when we get back to the hotel, you're the one reneging, not me."

He looks at her. "Are you being serious right now?"

"Look: I fully acknowledge I promised to do it in Eileen's bed tonight. But you can't *possibly* expect me to have sex among brain-eating ants."

"Of *course* not. It's okay. I don't want to do it in her bed either."

"Good. Now slap my back, will you?"

He does, then she slaps his.

"*Christ!*" she says.

"What's wrong?"

"I feel like they're crawling all over me! Are they in my *hair?* I feel like they're in my hair!"

"No."

"How can you tell? It's nearly pitch black out here."

"I'm sure we got out in time, but let's head back to the hotel. We can take a shower and check each other's bodies."

"Sounds good. After this, I'm gonna have nightmares forever."

"You'll be fine, I promise."

They get in the car, and Daisy starts the engine. "You realize we're no closer to finding Jake, right?"

"He's probably at the shack. We'll find him tomorrow."

"No offense, Bobby, but how can you stay *married* to that woman?" Before he can answer she adds: "You still think she's a nine?"

"Let's don't talk about her, okay?"

Chapter 23

AFTER A LONG, hot shower and a detailed body inspection, Daisy exits the bathroom wrapped in a full-length towel. A second, smaller one covers her hair like a turban. "Okay, I'm good," she says. "Your turn."

"Maybe I should check you more closely."

"No need. I scalded my body from top to bottom."

"What about your hair?"

"Double-scalded, combed, brushed. Plus, I checked my clothes, shoes, turned my handbag inside out, checked the lining and all the contents. I'm 100% free from infestation. And now—" She gestures to the shower: "—Your turn."

She walks past him to ready the bed. Within seconds he turns off the water and hollers, "All done!"

"Oh no, you're not! Do it again! And do it right this time."

Bobby showers a second time, towels dry, then stands in the doorway looking like a statue of a Roman god...after the Vandals desecrated its face. Ignoring Bobby's full-frontal nudity for the moment, Daisy pulls his head down and inspects his hair in the light.

Then she checks his body, front and back, paying special attention to his pubes.

"Want me to spread my cheeks?" he says, sarcastically.

"Yes."

As he turns and starts to, she says, "Stop! I was joking."

They move to his bed, which she's stripped to a single white sheet. "I checked," she says. "No ants."

As he sits on the end, facing her, she removes her turban and tosses her head, causing her hair to spill an inch below her shoulders. Bobby reaches toward her body towel, then hesitates. "Are there any rules I should know about?"

"Thanks for asking. Yes. I have two: first, that thing between your legs is enormous."

"Thank you."

"I don't mean it as a compliment. I like to think of sex as a pleasurable experience."

"It will be."

"Then go slowly."

"No problem. What's your second rule?"

"When we're done, don't lie to me."

"About what?"

"How good it was."

He frowns. "You're going in with low expectations?"

"I think it's the sensible way to proceed. I'd rather you were pleasantly surprised than bitterly disappointed."

"What if it turns out to be the best sex I ever had?"

"It won't. Good sex takes familiarity and practice. It's like making pancakes: you almost never get the first one right. But after that..."

"So...no pressure?"

"No pressure. We'll give it a shot and figure out what we like, and what we need to improve. Why are you smiling like that?"

"You're offering me a second chance before the first one starts!"

"Actually, I'm not. I'm just saying if this one sucks it's not necessarily a deal-killer. For me, at least."

"In that case, I officially apologize for every negative comment I've made about you."

"That apology covers a lot of ground. But thank you. I accept."

"Is this a good time to remove the towel?"

"It's the *perfect* time."

As he reaches to do so, a loud knock on the door startles them. "*Police! Open up! Right now, or we'll break down the door!*"

Chapter 24

BOBBY OPENS THE door and finds it's not the police at all. It's three guys wearing ski masks, and one has a gun that's already found a home in Bobby's ribs, forcing him to back up and sit on the bed.

If not for the calming effects of the drugs he ingested, Bobby's heart might be pounding out of his chest. But the more he focuses on the men, the less intimidating they seem. Daisy appears to agree, since her only reaction thus far has been nothing more than a raised eyebrow.

Bobby finds his alpha voice: "Who the fuck're you, and what do you want?"

"Let's not make this a *thing*," the third guy in the room says. "I'm Taggart. This is Charley, and the guy holding the gun on you is Elwood. We're not here to *hurt* you, but we'd *like* to."

Daisy says, "That's an odd thing to say."

Taggart shrugs. "It's like the end of days for guys like us. The whole area's experiencing a recession. People are becoming more tolerant of others. They're learning how to resolve petty disputes. Business is slow."

"Which business is that?" Bobby asks.

"They're leg-breakers," Daisy says. "Local. Small time."

"We prefer the term *enforcers*," Taggart says. "But the end result's the same. By the way, nice dick. What the hell must you have to do to get that thing inside her?"

Bobby's wondering the same thing, but what he says is, "Who hired you?"

Taggart ignores the question, walks to the nightstand, picks up a phone. "Who's is this?"

"Mine," Bobby says.

"Where's yours?" he asks Daisy.

She points to the opposite bed. "Under the pillow."

Taggart retrieves it and says, "Unlike your boyfriend, you don't appear to be the least bit rattled. I give you props for calling us small-time, since that's some strong shade to throw. And accurate, too, compared to some of the monsters that could've pulled the assignment. That said, it wouldn't be wise to underestimate us."

Bobby gives him a hard look. "Are you with Rocco or Vinny?"

"All will be revealed shortly."

"Why not now?"

"Is there a window in the bathroom?"

"No."

"Check it out, Charley. And while you're at it, make sure there are no weapons in there."

Moments later Charley emerges from the bathroom holding a switchblade and a gun. "I found these in her purse," he says.

"No window?"

Charley shakes his head.

Taggart says, "Miss, you may go to the bathroom unaccompanied to put some clothes on."

"Thank you."

"What's your name?"

"Daisy."

"My pleasure, Daisy. You may close the door, but please don't lock it."

Daisy stands, and looks at Bobby. "Are you okay?"

He nods.

When Daisy's in the bathroom, Taggart looks at Bobby and says, "I totally get the attraction. She's hotter than fire, spunky, and one-of-a-kind, like your Moon Pie. You think she might go out with me if I keep treating her nice?"

"No chance."

Taggart sighs. "Story of my life. Get dressed."

"Why?"

"Your pecker's freaking me out."

Charley laughs.

Bobby gets dressed, Daisy comes out, and Taggart motions her to sit on the bed.

"Let her go," Bobby says. "You can do whatever you want to me."

"Thank you, Bobby," Daisy says. "You're making progress."

Taggart smiles. "I love that. It's like he's giving me permission to hurt him, but only if I agree to his terms. But that's not how this business works, Bobby. Clearly, I can do whatever I want to *both* of you, and if I choose to be particularly vicious, there's not a thing in the world you'll be able to do about it." He sighs. "That said, I think you'd agree I've been respectful. I've certainly *tried* to establish rapport. I've showed restraint. And didn't I show good faith by allowing Daisy to get dressed in private?" He lets the question hang in the air and seems disappointed when neither of them responds. Eventually he says, "And now you're making demands."

He checks his watch and says, "So anyway, here's what's going to happen, and it's non-negotiable: Bobby, you're going for a ride with Elwood and Charley. Daisy, you're gonna stay here with me." When Bobby tenses up, Taggart says, "Don't be stupid, Bobby. At the moment you're not in any danger, and neither is Daisy. But that'll change in a heartbeat if you resist."

Daisy says, "You swear you won't hurt him?"

"I swear. Unless he tries something stupid."

"Where are you taking him?"

Taggart cocks his head. "Should I say?" He thinks it over. "Normally I wouldn't, but Bobby's getting tense, and I have no desire to cause either of you any undue stress or harm." He thinks about it some more, then says. "What the hell. I don't see any benefit to keeping you in the dark. They're gonna drive him to the woods to see his brother, Jake."

"Can I come?"

"Sorry. That's not part of the plan."

"My *brother* hired you?" Bobby says.

"That's correct. And he specifically said no harm should come to either of you, unless you resist. Elwood, that means if he tries something stupid in the car, shoot to wound, not kill."

"What if he gives me no choice?"

"In that case, shoot to kill. But look at me: that's a last resort, okay?"

Elwood nods.

Taggart says, "Bobby, stand up and put your hands behind your back so Charley can bind you with plastic ties."

When that's done Taggart says, "If Bobby gives you any trouble, call me, and I'll take my anger out on Daisy."

"That's not gonna happen," Bobby says. "I won't give them any reason to call you."

"Glad to hear it."

As the three men move toward the door, Daisy says, "I'm sorry Bobby."

"It's okay. I'll be fine."

"I meant, I'm sorry for everything Jake's gonna tell you about me."

Bobby stops, turns, shows a sad, pained expression. "You've been lying to me?"

She nods. "A little. But I was planning to tell you everything."

"When? After we fucked tonight?"

She scrunches her face. "No. I probably would've waited till we found Jake."

"The stuff I'm gonna hear: how bad is it?"

"Not as bad as it's gonna seem at first."

Bobby frowns. "Thanks for the warning."

He turns to leave. As they walk out the door, Daisy says, "Bobby? When this is all over, I'd like a chance to—"

"—To what, refute everything he tells me?"

"No. To explain."

He looks at her. "Of course."

"Thank you."

Chapter 25

THE THREE MEN leave the hotel room and walk down the steps. When they get to the car, Bobby gets in the backseat with Elwood, Charley takes the wheel. The sudden pinch in Bobby's arm tells him he's been injected with some sort of drug, and when he comes to, he's vaguely aware they're on a gravel road, which they follow about a mile or so before Charley parks the car by a stand of cypress trees. Charley flashes his lights, then cuts the power, and Bobby sits uneasily in the pitch-black middle of nowhere until a sudden knock on the opposite window startles him.

From the front seat, Charley clicks the unlock button. Elwood gets out and motions Bobby to slide across the seat and join him. When he does, he sees the face of the man that knocked on the window, illuminated by the car's interior.

As the hair rises on Bobby's neck, he works to keep the fear out of his voice.

"Who the fuck are *you?*" he asks, but the man says nothing. Just turns and starts walking in the dark. Elwood nudges Bobby with the gun and pushes him forward, letting him know they're supposed to follow. Bobby can't fathom how the guy in front of him can maneuver so effortlessly in the complete absence of light, and moments later, he and Elwood have lost him.

"Asshole!" Elwood mutters. He pulls a small pen light from his pocket, turns it on, and spots the man thirty yards in front of them, moving steadily. With the aid of the flashlight they're able to catch up, but after following him another hundred yards the man says, "Cut the flashlight."

"We can't see you," Elwood says.

"The grass is taller here. Just follow my sound and keep walking straight ahead for 200 steps."

They manage the distance without losing him, and when the man stops, they do the same. Moments later, a five-foot high by three-foot wide line of light is suddenly visible and Bobby realizes they're standing in front of the door of an enormous geodesic tent that's covered with layers of camouflage tarps. The man says, "You go in. We'll stand guard."

Bobby enters a tiny room that contains a camping table with chairs on either side. Bobby sits in the one that faces the interior door, and when it opens, Jake Cujo strolls in, takes one look at Bobby's face, and starts chuckling. "It's been a long time, but I can still recognize my baby brother under all those cuts and bandages!"

Bobby says, "Can you? Because you didn't seem to recognize the wedding ring on Eileen's finger when you stole her from me."

As Jake takes the opposite seat, Bobby adds, "Are you aware she's in the hospital?"

"I am. She's had a helluva time these last two months."

"She's got a fuckin' *ant* colony living in her head!"

"She does indeed. What's your opinion of Daisy?"

"Excuse me?"

"Have you banged her yet?"

Bobby cocks his head. "You've got nothing more to say about Eileen's condition? You *do* know who I'm talking about, right? My *wife*? The woman you *stole* from me?"

"You're repeating yourself, Bobby. If you care so much about Eileen, why'd you break into her house tonight instead of going to the hospital to check on her?"

Bobby frowns. "You had people *following* me?"

"Not you, specifically, but yes, I maintain constant video surveillance on her house, same as I do with your trailer."

"*What?*"

"I had hidden cameras placed throughout her house and your trailer. I monitor them from a station in this very structure."

"You've been *spying* on me? How long?"

"Months."

"That's bullshit."

"You require proof? Ask me something I shouldn't know."

Bobby eyes his older brother's face. "When Daisy and I left my trailer today, how was I dressed?"

"Exactly the way you are now, except for the ropes. She tied you up."

"That was too easy. One of your enforcers could have talked to Stacy or her daughter."

Jake says, "What about the two dead guys you left in your trailer?"

Chapter 26

"AGAIN, YOU COULD'VE got that information from Stacy or Cindy."

Jake smiles. "For a guy that claims Moon Pies resemble biblical characters, you're surprisingly skeptical."

"How about telling me something Stacy and Cindy *don't* know?"

"Here's one: after the True Believers left your trailer today you pulled your pants down, showed Daisy your dick, kissed her, put your hands down her jeans, and fainted when she pulled a wedding ring from her panties. Shall I continue?"

When Bobby says nothing, Jake adds: "The two guys you killed were gangsters from Miami. Tony and Eddie, if memory serves correct. You poisoned them, but Tony didn't die right away. Daisy killed him in your bed by sitting on his chest. I've got it all on tape. But don't worry about the dead guys, Little Brother. I've got a crew removing their bodies even as we speak. By the way, you're welcome."

It takes Bobby a half-minute to react, as he mentally sifts through all the shit he's done in that trailer over the past few months completely unaware he was being watched.

Jake says, "I wasn't snooping, I've been protecting you. I felt an obligation to keep you and Eileen safe, since I'm the one who put your lives in danger by refusing to work with the mob."

"Where's Julie? Did you have anything to do with her disappearance?"

Jake sighs. "There *is* no Julie."

"Don't *lie* to me!"

"Look, Bobby, I know you like Daisy, and who wouldn't? She's pure adrenalin! But she's not who you think she is." Jake flashes a warm smile. "I *do* care about you, Little Brother, but..." He sighs. "You've done it again."

"Done what?"

"Fallen in love with the wrong woman."

"You're insane."

"And you're a hopeless romantic. It's your Kryptonite."

"I have no idea what you're talking about."

"I know you don't, so let me say it simply: we're both attracted to the same type of women, but we have different opinions on how to keep them happy. And yours is wrong."

"How so?"

"The secret to keeping a woman happy isn't romance, it's doubt."

Bobby rolls his eyes.

"Bear with me, Little Brother. You and I are attracted to gorgeous women who require two things from a relationship: security and challenge. And they try to get it from two types of guys: Dogs and Lions."

Bobby laughs. "I always wondered what people think about when they're isolated for long periods of time."

"Good one. But hear me out: women tell themselves they want a romantic guy who'll treat them like a princess. But you know from personal experience that the better you treat her the worse she'll treat you."

"Is there a short version of this life lesson? Be sure to include the dogs and lions."

"No problem. Men are typically either Dogs or Lions. The Dog offers security, loyalty, friendship, and unconditional love."

"Sounds great. Sign me up."

"I know, right? And that's why every mom and dad prays their daughter will marry a Dog. Sadly, the daughter can't help but notice the Lions lurking about. Slightly outside her comfort zone, they offer challenge, excitement, and danger."

"Let's wrap this up, okay?"

"Sure. When the relationship is new, she can't believe how incredible you are. No one ever treated her so well. But over time, when she knows she's *got* you, she loses interest. Know why?"

"Because she requires a challenge?"

"Exactly. Maybe it took some time, but she finally turned you into the Dog. And now that she has the *security* she needs, she's ready to focus on the *challenge*. So she starts noticing the Lions who've been lurking about. Women are naturally attracted to high-profile, confident men they consider slightly unattainable: men who demand—and are therefore *worthy*—of their full attention. While seeking this 'better man' she'll criticize you, stop having sex with you, and she'll eventually cheat on you. Sound familiar?"

"Fuck you!"

"A woman's mind and body are constantly at war. Her brain wants the security the Dog provides, but her body wants the Lion: a man she can't predict or control. She wants to fuck men who are exciting, dangerous, and a step above her—not the guy who worships her, deals with her bullshit, and pays her bills. Because *that* guy's a step below her."

"I wasn't Eileen's Dog."

"Not at first. Then again, no guy starts out as the Dog. If we did, we'd never have a chance." He smiles. "We start out as Puppies: cute, adorable, fun. In the early days, Eileen loved hanging out with you. Wanted to spend all her time with you. Showed you off to all her friends. But after the newness wears off, Puppies grow up and become Dogs, and that's what happened to you."

"Women love dogs."

"Absolutely! Dogs are steady, and predictable. They wait at the door for her return and lap up any bit of affection the she bestows on them. But women don't fuck their dogs. They give them head pats and table scraps. And if they decide to bring a new Puppy into the household, what's the Dog going to do about it? Leave? No way! Why? Because he's a Dog!"

"So, I'm supposed to be the Lion? That's your advice?"

"No. Lions offer excitement, but not security. Women want to marry the Dog and fuck the Lion, but it never works out. Thankfully, there exists a third type of man."

"Let me guess: it's you, the Wolf in sheep's clothing."

"Funny. Actually, it's me, the Fox. The Fox gives her a taste of security, but never lets her get comfortable. She wants him to be less Lion, more Dog, but he only gives her just enough of each."

"Got it all figured out, have you?"

"Just that part."

"Well, this might surprise you, Jake, but I have zero interest in your love life. You suddenly act like you *care* about me? You stole my fucking *wife*!"

"There it is again, and yes I did. And it pained me greatly. But what you *don't* know is Eileen and I were in a serious relationship when you met her."

"That's a complete and utter lie!"

"Think about it, Bobby: you didn't find *her*, she found *you*. "Eileen and I were *living* together. We had a great thing going, but I cheated, and she moved out, refused my calls, and started harassing the young lady I was seeing. Then, for revenge, she started dating you."

Red-faced, Bobby says, "That's the most self-serving, narcissistic comment I've ever heard in my life. Eileen *loved* me. If she hadn't, she wouldn't have *married* me."

"I agree she loved you. But the reason she pursued you was to punish me. It was that whole '*Cheat on me? Well, I fucked your brother!*' dynamic. But somewhere along the way she fell in love with the *idea* of you, because—as she said numerous times—no one would ever love her like Bobby Cujo. After dating me, you were a welcome relief. And when you proposed she got swept up in the emotion and said yes, only to change her mind in the weeks before the ceremony."

"What are you *talking* about?"

"In the weeks before the wedding, Eileen called me day and night, said she was about to make the biggest mistake of her life. But just as she was about to break things off she learned that all the wedding deposits her parents had paid were non-refundable. She couldn't bear to hurt you and disappoint and embarrass them, so she went through with the ceremony. At the reception, she and I had a long talk. We agreed she'd never find a guy who'd treat her as well as you, and she made an oath to try as hard as she could to make the marriage work. And I honestly think she tried. But in the end, she was miserable."

"And that's when you swooped in."

"Well, obviously, I could have kept turning her away, but you know damn well she would have found someone else. And the truth is, I never stopped loving her."

"Then why isn't she with you?"

"Look around, Bobby. I live in a tent on the edge of a swamp."

"If you loved her, you'd want to *be* with her. If you *loved* her, you wouldn't have *cheated* on her."

"There it is again: your romantic notion of love. For you it's cut and dry, but my affairs serve two purposes: they're fun for me and they keep Eileen from getting complacent. Which would *you* rather have: a woman who treats you like a Dog? Or an angry girlfriend who hopes if she treats you even *better* tonight, maybe you won't cheat on her tomorrow?"

"Neither. Because both are warped Did you even bother to *ask* her if she'd be willing to live like this?"

"I did. How do you think the ants got in her head?"

Chapter 27

JAKE SAYS, "WHEN I saw dead ants in her ear I sent her back to Plaquemine so she could meet with doctors and get treatment."

"You put her in harm's way with the mob."

"I didn't have a choice. But for her protection, we hatched a plan: she found some rich schlub on a dating site and started a public relationship. She'll keep that romance going until her medical issue's resolved. In the meantime, we stay in touch."

"How?"

"I'd rather not say."

"There were no messages between you and Eileen on her computer. Daisy checked."

"Nevertheless..."

"You also said there are hidden cameras in Eileen's house. I don't think so. I would've seen them."

"Clearly, you didn't. But if you want to locate the ones in your trailer, wait till it's dark, turn off the lights, and aim a flashlight around the room till you see a little sparkle. That's the back-flash that occurs when light hits the camera lens."

Bobby frowns. "I hope you got a thrill out of watching my dates use the bathroom."

"It wasn't like that."

"Yes, it was, and it proves what an asshole you are. And if you're telling the truth, Eileen's no better. According to you, she purposely went online and found this David Cage guy and made phony advances to him, the same way she came on to me."

"Same idea, different execution. And yes, she's just as bad as me, and possibly *worse*, since I wouldn't have pursued her sister if Eileen cheated on me. But you're right in saying she and I use others to get what we want."

"In other words, you're perfect for each other."

"I'm glad you finally understand."

"So, what's the plan, Jake? You gonna live in a tent the rest of your life?"

"Not at all. We have alternate names and passports. When Eileen gets better we're going to leave the country and start a new life together."

"That's the type of information the mob could beat out of me."

"True. Which is why I want *you* to leave the country too."

"I'm not gonna live with you and Eileen!"

Jake laughs. "Nor would I *want* you to, given her predilection for revenge fucking. But Tony and Eddie proved you're no longer safe at your trailer, so you need to go *somewhere*. If you're willing to leave the country, I can help you."

"How?"

"I've set aside a million dollars for you."

"*Excuse me?*"

"In certain areas, it's enough money to live like a king for the rest of your life."

"A million dollars?"

Jake nods.

Bobby blinks several times. Then says, "Where would I have to go?"

"You'd have endless choices. But you need to get your head straight first."

"What do you mean?"

"You need to ditch Daisy."

"Why?"

"How many reasons do you need?"

"Three."

"One, she's dangerous. Two, she's crazy. And three, you're in love with her, which means you're already the Dog."

"I'll say it again: I barely know her. It's been exactly one day."

"For you, one day's more than enough. It's also long enough to know she's crazy."

"If by crazy you're referring to Julie, where's your proof?"

"When I say Daisy's crazy, I don't mean it in a casual way. She has serious psychological issues. But don't take my word for it, run a background check. You'll find no reference to Julie, because she exists only in Daisy's mind. If you think *that's* weird, wait till you're in the same room when she and Julie are *talking*, and both voices are coming from Daisy's mouth."

"Tell me again how you know so much about Daisy?"

"She used to be my bookkeeper."

"She said Julie was your bookkeeper."

"Ask her again, now that she knows we've talked."

"I don't believe you."

"You *never* believe me!"

"How *could* I? You stole my fucking *wife!*"

"*This* again? Jesus, Bobby, I'm trying to *help* you."

"Prove it. Tell me what you know about Daisy."

Jake takes a deep breath. "Let's start with this: the woman you know as Daisy Pepper was born Leah Shea. And if she's dating Vinny the Prick, the relationship can't be more than two weeks old. Also, she helped me embezzle $3 million from my own company. And, uh... brace yourself: Daisy and I have been seeing each other for more than a year."

Chapter 28

"*SEEING* EACH OTHER? What does *that* mean?"

"It means we've been having sex, Bobby."

"What about Eileen?"

"Same answer."

Bobby grits his teeth. "How is it you keep fucking my women?"

"I could ask *you* the same question, since I dated *both* of them before *you* did. By the way, I noticed you weren't surprised when I said her name was Leah Shea. Why's that?"

Bobby looks down. Murmurs, "It's not important."

Jake says, "You're me, ten months ago, including the face. We were out one night, our second or third date. I told her to pick the activity, and figured she'd say dinner and a movie or something, but she wanted to go to a *biker* bar!" He laughs. "After a couple of drinks, she picked a fight with three offshore oil riggers, and by the time I finished defending her honor, I looked exactly like you do right now." As he thinks about it, a smile curls his lips. "I swear, Bobby: Leah's the most exciting woman I ever met."

"Her name's Daisy."

"Right. And by the way, it's her legal name now, which is why I'm surprised she'd use an old credit card. Have you slept with her yet?"

"That's none of your business."

Jake nods. "Well, bang her tonight while you can, 'cause I guarantee she'll be the best fuck of your life."

"I'm sure Eileen would be thrilled to hear you say that."

"As I said earlier, I love Eileen, and always will. But her finest qualities—as I'm sure you know—are showcased outside the bedroom. As for Daisy? Bang her tonight, then put her out of your mind. Because falling in love with the wrong woman turned out to be a disaster for you last time, and trust me, Daisy will be far worse. Do yourself a favor: walk away."

"No."

Jake shakes his head. "Well, it's your life to live. All I can do is offer advice, and I have. As before, I'll wish you all the best. Are you ready to go?"

"If you've been seeing her for the past year, why doesn't she know where you are?"

"I dumped her. Didn't want to, but I couldn't take both her *and* Eileen out of the country."

"How positive are you that Julie doesn't exist?"

"One hundred percent."

"Does Daisy know?"

"Great question! Probably not. There's got to be some sort of trigger event that launches the imaginary missing sister, but I have no clue what it is. On the bright side, it never lasts long."

"Did she study blue coral snakes?"

"Yes, and she *loves* them. Well, loves their venom, at least. Have you ever seen a photo of a blue coral?"

"No."

"Absolutely stunning. A gorgeous species."

"Is she smart?"

"She's brilliant."

"Where'd you meet her, Tulane?"

"Yeah, but she went there after I graduated. Majored in Herpetology, Ecology, and Evolutionary Biology. Out of 90,000 specimens on display at Tulane, she fell in love with the blue coral snake, and hoped to work for a major pharmaceutical company to research its venom. But she only had a partial scholarship, and needed a job."

"If she's so brilliant why couldn't she get a full scholarship?"

"She didn't apply till she was twenty."

"Why not?"

"After college, she moved to Brooklyn to save her father's pizza business."

"How'd you meet her?"

"She attended a lecture and I was one of the speakers. I was thirty-three, a multi-millionaire, single. After the lecture, she introduced herself and asked if I had any part-time positions available. We discussed it over dinner and sex, and I rewarded her with a part-time job in my office, and she turned out to be extremely competent. I told her after graduating she could work full-time as my personal assistant."

"And she did?"

"Yeah. But a few months later the mob showed up, killed Sully, and forced me to give up control. When they started selling off the assets we needed to survive, I fired my office staff, put Daisy in charge of the corporate checkbook, and taught her how to siphon money into phony accounts by making payments to non-existent vendors. Then I disappeared and I guess she went back to Brooklyn and hooked up with Vinny the Prick."

"When was this?"

"About two weeks ago, give or take."

"And now she's back? Why?"

Jake laughs. "I expect she wants the quarter million bucks I promised her."

"Why not pay her?"

"I decided to keep it for myself."

"But she helped you get it."

"True, but it was my money in the first place. Bear in mind, last year I owned a $40 million company. Now I'm on the run, with $3 million. And I'm giving you a third of *that*."

"If you promised her a quarter million, you need to pay it."

"It's not like she made *nothing* all those months. She was paid extremely well."

"If she's dating Vinny dePazzio it could be bad for you."

"Yeah, but even worse for *you*. Which is why you need to get the fuck outta Dodge. Are you ready to go back to the hotel?"

"What about my million dollars?"

Chapter 29

JAKE SMILES. "THAT'S my boy. Your money's in a numbered account, overseas." He reaches into his pocket, pulls out an ink pen and a business card. "Memorize this guy's name and number, then destroy the card. He's your contact."

"Then what?"

"At your earliest convenience, like tomorrow morning, make sure your passport's up-to-date. Then destroy your cell phone, buy some burner phones, and book a flight to London, Paris, or Hong Kong. When you arrive, call your contact, and he'll tell you where to get your new ID and bank account. When that's done, he'll wire the money and you'll be off and running."

"Where are *you* going?"

"I can't tell you. But if you'd like a recommendation, two of my top three places were the Algarve coast of Portugal, and Las Terrenas, in the Dominican Republic." Jake uses the pen to write the names on the back of the card. Then says, "I hate to bring this up, but taking Daisy would be a huge risk. She could clean you out within a week. Not to mention, she'll want to live in Bangkok so she can research her snakes."

"Like I said, I've only known her since this morning. I doubt she's ready to renounce her citizenship."

"It should go without saying, but don't show her the contact information I gave you."

"I'm not stupid."

"*You're* not, but *Love* is. Anyway, I know she drove you here in her rental car. I'll have Elwood and Charley drive you back home. Do you want to stop by the hotel first?"

"Yeah. But I can get home on my own."

Jake shrugs. "Your choice. But check on Eileen before you leave town."

"Why?"

"It'll establish your alibi in case someone sees my guys removing bodies from your trailer."

"I've already got an alibi: the hotel, remember?"

"You checked in with Leah's credit card."

"Yeah, but the desk clerk saw me."

"Totally unreliable. He probably couldn't pick you out of a lineup. Be smart: go to the hospital. Talk to the nurses, the doctor, and Eileen, if she's awake."

Jake reaches into his pocket and hands Bobby a wad of cash. "This should cover your airfares and any expenses you'll have until your money's available."

"Thanks."

"Please don't be offended, but we'll need to renew your sedative when you get back in the car."

"I expected no less."

Jake gives him a long look. "This is probably the last time we'll ever see each other, Bobby. I may not be your favorite person, but I've always cared about you. I hope you have a wonderful life."

Bobby gets to his feet. "You too."

As Jake moves closer to embrace him, Bobby punches him in the jaw, as hard as he can.

Chapter 30

NOW, IN THE hotel parking lot, Bobby jerks himself conscious, hears Elwood say, "You awake yet, Sleeping Ugly?"

"Yeah."

"It's about fuckin' time. Let's go see how Taggart and Daisy are doing."

The three men exit the car, walk past Daisy's car, climb the stairs to the second floor, and walk down the hall to Daisy and Bobby's room. After a brief knock that goes unanswered, Charley chuckles. "Maybe they're fucking."

Elwood uses the key to gain entrance, and when he opens the door what they see isn't fucking. They all gasp, but Charley's the one who verbalizes it:

Chapter 31

"TAGGART'S DEAD!"

Both men grab their guns. While Charley trains his on Bobby, Elwood moves toward the closed bathroom door and says, "Come on out, Bitch. Time to face the music."

Getting no response, Elwood turns sideways to make himself a smaller target. Then reaches for the door knob, turns it, and...

The bathroom's empty.

"Fuck!"

They stare at Taggart's body in horror. He's lying face down on the bed with his pants and underwear around his ankles. Most disturbing is the blood and bile in the crack of his ass and the puddle of blood that cascaded down the back of his balls and pooled on the bed beneath them.

"What the fuck did she *do* to him?" Charley says. "It looks like she reached deep into his asshole and pulled it inside out!"

"Search his pockets," Elwood says.

"Fuck you!" Charley says. "I'm the driver. *You* search his pockets!"

Elwood does, then glances around the room and comes to the conclusion Daisy stole Taggart's phone, wallet, and both guns: his own, and the one he confiscated from her two hours earlier.

Charley says, "Well, *that* was stupid!"

"What was?"

"Taking his phone. We can track her off the cell towers."

"Oh yeah? Do it."

"Huh?"

"Start tracking her."

"Well, I mean, *I* don't know how to do it, but on TV—"

"Are we on TV?"

"No."

"Then shut the fuck up."

Charley says, "She can't have gotten very far. Her car's still here."

Elwood shakes his head. "That bitch is long gone."

"What do you mean?"

"How long did we sit in the parking lot waiting for this bastard to wake up just now? Half an hour? She left the car here so we wouldn't be suspicious." He thinks a minute. "She probably watched us the whole time, and—"

They look at each other.

"Shit!" Elwood runs out of the room, down the hall, down the steps, flings the exit door open and sees exactly what he expected:

Daisy's car is gone.

What he didn't expect to see were the four slashed tires on *Charley's* car.

Chapter 32

ACCORDING TO HIS driver's license, Earl Taggart's home is located fourteen miles away, in White Castle. When Daisy knocks on the door and puts a gun in his wife's face she says, "He ain't here."

"I know. Take five steps back."

"There ain't nothin' to steal, Miss. An eighth of weed, maybe, but that's about it."

"Five steps back. I won't ask you again."

"Sorry," she says. "You woke me out of a deep sleep."

Mrs. Taggart takes five steps back, and Daisy follows her inside, closes the door behind her, and looks around the room. "Who else lives here?"

"My girl."

"How old is she?"

"Fifteen."

"Where is she?"

"In her bedroom, fuckin' her boyfriend."

"You let that happen in your own home?"

"If I don't, they'll fuck on the levee. You ever fucked on the levee?"

"Once, in college."

"Well, if you did it near here, you know how dangerous it is. A guy once tore the door off a car to get to the girl inside." She shudders, and crosses herself before saying, "That was years ago, and they *still* talk about what he done to her." She glances down the hall. "That's unusual."

"What is?"

"It's quiet. They must be sleepin' or smokin' pot. They crank up the music when fuckin', so I won't hear her holler. What do you want with me?"

"Information about your husband's boss, Jake Cujo."

"Like what?"

"You know where Jake's hiding?"

"Why the fuck should I tell you?"

"Because I'll kill you if you don't."

Mrs. Taggart looks at Daisy, then at the gun she's holding. "No offense, honey, but you don't look like no kind of killer to me. You even know how to *use* that thing?"

While holding the gun in her right hand, Daisy fishes through her purse with her left till she finds Earl's wallet, which she hands to Mrs. Taggart.

"Where'd you get it?" she asks, wide-eyed.

"Same place I got *this*," Daisy says, holding up Taggart's phone. "What's your name?"

"Lucille Taggart."

"Well Lucille, I'm looking for answers, and I don't have much time. Where's Jake Cujo hiding?"

"He'll kill me if I tell."

"Who will? Jake?"

"No. My husband, Earl."

Lucille's house is larger than it appeared from the street, with lots of open space. From the foyer, where they're standing, Daisy can see the kitchen, dining room, two hallways, and a small living room. She gestures toward the dining room: "Maybe you should sit down."

Lucille does, and Daisy accesses a photo on Earl's phone before handing it to her. "Is that Earl?"

"*Jesus! Omigod!* What *happened* to him?"

"There was an incident."

"No shit there was!" Lucille says. She takes a surprisingly short time to compose herself. "Did you *kill* him?"

"Let's just say I was there when it happened."

"Well, thank God! I been prayin' for this for years. How'd it go down?"

"He held a gun on me and threatened to kill me. No offense, but I offered him a blow job to let me go."

"Well, who wouldn't? But how'd you dynamite his asshole?"

"Earl said no to the blow job, but then he winked at me and said, 'You know what I *really* like?'"

Lucille clucks. "Oh Lord, I can see where *this* is goin'."

"He wanted me to tongue his ass."

She nods, then stares at the photo some more. "What's your tongue *made* of, *razor* blades?"

"While Earl pulled his pants down I snuck a vial of snake venom from my handbag. Then I spread his cheeks and poured it in him and pushed the vial into his ass for good measure."

"Did it hurt?"

"What do *you* think?"

"I bet it did."

"You'd win that bet. The hardest part was muffling his screams."

"How'd you manage it?"

"Being face down and suffering, Earl lost his grip on his gun. I grabbed it and smashed the back of his head and knocked him out, and the venom did the rest. You don't seem too upset at the news."

"You have any idea how many bruises, broken bones, and busted lips that man gave me? Too many to count." She looks down at the floor. "And that whole *ass-lickin'* thing?" She winces. "I never got that. But I'll tell you this much: it's a taste that don't go away on its own." She looks up at Daisy. "You know he never would've let you go, right?"

Daisy nods.

"And you wouldn't have been the first, neither. You were smart to kill him."

"The venom killed him. I just introduced it."

"When do you think I can call to collect on the insurance?"

"After you receive official notice."

"When will *that* be?"

"Soon, if Charley and Elwood don't hide his body somewhere."

Lucille looks concerned. "If they do, I'll never collect! You need to call 911 and tell 'em where he's at."

"I'll tell you after you tell me where Jake is."

"I truly don't know."

"You must know *something.*"

Lucille hesitates, then says, "All right, but you didn't hear this from me, okay?"

Daisy nods.

Lucille says, "Earl was bad enough. I don't need no *worse* men comin' around askin' questions over what I said or didn't say about where Jake Cujo's hidin' out. You understand the kind of men who'd want to know the answers to them questions?"

"I do. And I promise your name won't come up. You have my word."

"If they ask how you found out, what'll you say?"

"I'll say I forced Earl to tell me before he died."

Lucille nods. "Okay. I reckon that'll work."

"Where's Jake?"

Lucille lowers her voice. "I don't know how current this is, but a couple weeks ago I heard Earl complainin' to Charley that him and Elwood and some other guy were helpin' Jake in the woods near Bayou Pierre, east of Gonzales."

"What were they helping Jake do?"

"Move his tent mansion."

"His *what?*"

"Well, *mansion* ain't the right word. But it's a big-ass tent, and Earl was pissed 'cause it took four men two days to move it to the new location, along with all Jake's electronic equipment. He said the tent had a giant dome. He called it a G-dome, or somethin' like that."

"Geodesic dome?"

"That sounds right, but don't quote me. All Earl said was, it's huge."

"Ought to be easy to see from the air."

"You'd think so, but they got it covered with camo tarps."

"What's Charley's last name?"

"Wake."

"Is he married?"

Lucille nods. "Lorna works at the high school."

"You know their address?"

"They're in Donaldsonville. I went there once. Don't know the address, but it's a white house with a red door." She ponders it a few seconds. "Seems like the street they're on was named after a flower, but I ain't positive. I know they live close to the high school, 'cause he don't let her use the car."

Suddenly, they hear loud music from a room down the hallway. "Now they're fuckin'," she says. "Lordy mercy, I can't wait to tell her!"

"Your daughter?"

"Uh huh."

"Won't she be upset?"

"Oh, *hell* no! Earl weren't her daddy. He's just the bastard that made our lives miserable all these years. The only good thing that man ever did was check the box for paid-up life insurance durin' them six years he worked on the oil rig. I swear, Miss, you done us a service. We can put that twenty grand to good use."

"Glad I could help."

Lucille says, "So, where'd you leave his body?"

Daisy tells her the hotel and room number, then says goodbye and starts walking across the lawn toward the street. As she approaches her car, she hears a gunshot behind her. She freezes, then turns to see Lucille standing in the front yard, illuminated by the porch light, aiming a handgun at her face. "That there was a warnin' shot," Lucille barks. "Don't take another step, or it'll be your last. Now drop your purse and put your hands in the air, and we'll call 911 together."

Daisy does as she's told, and Lucille starts walking toward her. When she gets ten feet away she removes her phone from her back pocket and dials 911. Daisy hears the operator say: "Nine-one-one, what's your emergency?"

And Lucille says...

Actually, Lucille grunts and falls to the ground, and Daisy knows why: according to scientific studies, a 9mm bullet fired straight into the sky will travel approximately 4,000 feet and require approximately 37 seconds to come back to Earth. Depending on a host of variables, including velocity, motion, air density, and gravitational pull—the bullet will arc slightly, then return to earth tumbling at speeds between 300 and 700 feet per second, which is fast enough to penetrate a person's skull. Those of you who are skeptical need to look no further than the bloody entrance wound at the top of Lucille's head, and watch the final twitching of her body. Daisy does so with interest, then lowers her arms, picks up her purse, gets in her car, and drives away.

Chapter 33

LUCILLE WAS RIGHT: Charley and Lorna's white house with a red door is located near the high school on one of three streets named after a flower. She assumed Charley's car wouldn't be in the carport yet, and it's not.

Daisy takes several photos of Charley's house, texts them to Vinny, along with his address, then drives to an all-night gas station and fills her tank using her Leah Shea credit card.

She's worried about Bobby.

When he left the hotel with Elwood and Charley she figured Jake would tell him everything and she'd never see him again. But then she killed Taggart, and now Bobby's life could be in danger. It was a stupid thing to do, but Taggart gave her no choice after threatening to blackmail her. Although Rocco has no idea Jake's company was embezzled, somehow Taggart knew, and said if she didn't party with him in the hotel tonight and give him a cut of the money tomorrow, he'd tell Rocco everything, including how to find Jake.

Knowing she's way out of her league with these professional killers, Daisy used the venom on Taggart, then made the tough decision to turn the job of finding Jake over to Vinny. The problem is, Vinny will almost certainly cheat her out of her fifty percent.

But at least she'll be alive.

Daisy took Taggart's wallet and phone, packed her suitcase, and put it in the trunk of her car. Then she hid in the parking lot and waited for Elwood and Charley to return, and surprisingly, Bobby was with them. After slashing Charley's tires, Daisy fled the scene, terrified that Jake would tell his men to kill Bobby after forcing him to help them clean the hotel room and dispose of Earl's body.

Daisy wants to warn him, but she also needs to get somewhere safe, because if Taggart knew about the embezzlement, someone else probably knows. Since the hotel room was purchased in her *old* name, and she's now known as Daisy Pepper, she wonders if this is a good time to start using the new identity she purchased in Bangkok two weeks ago, while waiting for Jake to arrive.

Now, heading north on I-55 to Jackson, Mississippi, she gets a call. Expecting it to be Vinny, she automatically says, "Sorry to wake you."

But it's not Vinny, it's Bobby. And he says:

Chapter 34

"I WASN'T ASLEEP. Are you somewhere safe?"

"I'm working on it. What about you?"

"I'm good."

In the background, Charley hollers, "Tell that bitch she owes me four new tires!"

"Sorry about the outburst," Bobby says. "But he's got a point. Why'd you slash his tires?"

"Why do you *think*? I didn't want them following me! Listen, Bobby, you need to get away from those guys. I think they're gonna kill you."

Bobby laughs. "*You're* the only killer *I* know. Jesus, Daisy, what'd you do to Taggart?"

"Kept him from killing *me*. Where are you right now?"

"At the hospital."

"Are you hurt?"

"Naw, I'm just checking on Eileen to establish an alibi while Jake's enforcers get the bodies out of my trailer. Jake wants Charley and Elwood to drive me home tonight, but I was hoping you and I could stay here in town, spend the night together, and drive back

133

tomorrow. Otherwise, I'll have to help Elwood with his job, then ride all night back to the trailer."

"First of all, it's nearly daybreak. Second, this *job* you mentioned: does it involve dumping Earl's body?"

"No. Jake's taking care of that. You still have my Moon Pie?"

"Bobby, focus: these men are dangerous. I know for a fact Earl Taggart was a killer. His wife *admitted* it."

"I know. Elwood and Charley admitted it, too. But most of Jake's crew are normal guys. Charley's a valve salesman, and Elwood runs a vending route. That's the job I'd have to help him with if you don't come get me."

"How are you able to make this call?"

"What do you mean?"

"Why are they allowing you to call me?"

"They're hoping you'll take me home tomorrow so they won't have to drive me tonight."

"Sorry, Buddy. I'm long gone."

He sighs. "I was afraid you were gonna say that."

In the background, she hears Elwood's voice: "What'd she say?"

"She said she's long gone."

"Shit."

Now Elwood's talking to Charley: "Why do *I* have to come? Why can't *you* drive him?"

Charley says: "I've been up twenty-two hours already. I can't drive all the way to his trailer and back safely."

Bobby says, "Hey Charley? I can drive you and me back to my trailer and you can sleep in the car. If you're still tired when we get there, you can crash at my place for a few hours."

Daisy listens as Charley says, "That'll work. But if Elwood's not comin', he can run his own damn vendin' route."

Elwood says, "Perfect. But clear it with Jake."

134

Bobby says, "Guys? Can you give me a minute to talk to Daisy in private?"

When they're gone, Bobby's voice goes low. "Daisy? I've got a good feeling about us. Can you hear me okay?"

"Yes."

"Good. Because I've got a proposition for you."

"Bobby, look: I'm sorry if I've given you the wrong impression, but—"

"Please: hear me out. How much money would you need to start researching those blue coral snakes?"

"What are you talking about?"

"Jake set aside a bunch of money so I could leave the country and start a new life. And I'd like you to come with me."

"Excuse me?"

"It could be a great opportunity for you. We could move to Bangkok and I'd give you the money to start your research."

"Is this a joke?"

"Not at all. Like I said, I've got a good feeling about us."

She sighs loud enough for Bobby to hear it. Then says, "Was Bangkok Jake's idea?"

"No. Well...he *did* mention that's where you'd probably want to go if I took you. And I'd like to, so what do you say?"

"You told Jake you wanted to take me?"

"Yeah, absolutely."

"And that was okay with him?"

"Yeah. I mean, he warned me about a few things, but in the end he said it was my life to live."

"What did he say about me? If he told the truth, there's no way you'd want to see me again."

"It wasn't so bad. He said your real name's Leah Shea, and you guys have been sleeping together for the past year and you helped him steal three million dollars from his company."

"And you're okay with all that?"

"I'm not saying it's *ideal*, but everything you did happened before you met me, so yeah, I can handle it."

"Did he happen to mention the recent trip I took?"

"Are you talking about Brooklyn?"

"No. That was *this* week. Two weeks ago I went to Bangkok."

"*What?*"

"Bangkok, Thailand. That's where I got the snake venom I used to kill Taggart."

"You went there alone?"

"As it turned out, yes. But Jake was supposed to meet me there. Are you ready for this? We were gonna start a new life together."

"I don't understand."

"I embezzled six million, not three, and Jake promised me half. The last time I saw him was six weeks ago. He was going to Thailand to set everything up. We were gonna buy a pharmaceutical company and produce pain remedies from blue coral venom. We were also planning to hire Philippian scientists to work on a cheap version of Zohydro. You know what that is?"

"Not really."

"It's a pain medication made from hydrocodone bitartrate that has ten times the abuse potential of OxyContin. It's about to be approved in America soon, so stay away from that shit. Anyway, that was the plan: Jake was gonna go there first, to set things up, and I was gonna fly there a month later. He was gonna come back to America, to set up some distribution channels, then fly to Bangkok, and meet me at the airport. But he shafted me. So, I made a deal with Vinny to help me get my share."

"Jake said he promised you a quarter million, but changed his mind, and you guys broke up because he wanted to be with Eileen. They're moving somewhere overseas."

"Did he say when?"

"He said they'd be there now, if it weren't for her medical problems."

"Did he say where they're going?"

"No."

"I don't expect you to believe this, but Jake told me he loved me, and that I was the only woman in his life. He said the reason we had to stop dating and spending the nights together these last few months was because it would call attention to our relationship, and they might suspect we were stealing money."

"Jake's a womanizer. Of course I believe you."

"Thanks. I know you're developing feelings for me, but until two weeks ago my whole world revolved around Jake and our plans for the future. The first time I heard Eileen's name was this morning, when you dropped that bombshell on me."

"I gotta say, you handled it really well."

"Thanks. But the fact she's your wife? You handled *that* better than *I* would've."

Neither of them speaks for a full minute. Bobby finally says, "You're so much better off not having Jake in your life. But don't close the door yet on us. I can't give you three million, but I can share the million he's giving me. And that doesn't even count the cash he gave me tonight."

"Oh, Bobby..."

"What?"

"Don't you get it? Jake didn't put any money aside for you. He just wants you out of the country."

"Why?"

"I think he's trying to protect you from the mob. But Jake's not the type to give away a million bucks, even to you. How much did you get tonight?"

"Six grand."

"Well, use it wisely, 'cause I expect that's all you're gonna get."

"I'll admit Jake's an asshole where women are concerned, but I'm the only family he has. I think he's serious about the million."

"Do you? Reason I ask, he's been a multi-millionaire for years. How many checks has he sent you?"

"None."

"Then why start now?"

"Because I'm the only family he has, and he's never going to see me again."

"How was he gonna transfer the money?"

"He gave me a phone number to his contact. When I land in Europe, I'm supposed to call the guy and he'll tell me where to set up an account. Then he'll wire the money."

"Call him tonight."

"Huh?"

"In two hours the banks will be open in Europe. Don't fly all the way there to get shafted. Call the guy tonight and tell him you want the money in your personal account here in the States. See what he says."

"And if he sends it, will you go with me?"

"No."

"Why not?"

"How many reasons do you need?"

"At least three."

"First, it's not enough money. Second, I'd have to love you, and I don't. And third, I'm still hoping to get the money Jake owes me."

"Can I ask you something?"

"Of course."

"Do you still love him?"

Chapter 35

DAISY SAYS, "YOU'VE heard about that fine line between love and hate? Well, Jake crossed it."

"You're sure you're over him?"

"Completely. It'd be one thing if he just stood me up in Thailand after promising to marry me. Or if he just had an affair. Or if he left me for another woman. Or if he did nothing more than talk me into committing a crime. Or if he put my life in danger. Or if he promised to give me $3 million and shafted me. But Jake did *all* of those things."

"I know you don't love me yet, but you should come with me anyway. We can use the million dollars to buy a company. If we work hard we can build it up, sell it, and earn enough to start your pharmaceutical company."

She laughs. "This morning your dream was to have a Moon Pie museum. Now you want to start a pharmaceutical company in a country where you don't even speak the language."

"If Jake can do it, I can do it."

"No offense, Bobby, but that's not even remotely true. Look: if you're certain Elwood and Charley aren't gonna kill you tonight,

139

drive home. In two hours, call the contact guy and tell him to wire the money to your local account first thing tomorrow morning. If there's no money, you saved yourself the hassle of a one-way trip overseas."

"What about my Moon Pie?"

"I'll send it to you tomorrow by overnight mail."

"What about the cash from the hospital?"

"Keep it all, with my blessing."

"What will *you* do for money?"

"I still have the $50,000 Jake gave me."

"*Excuse* me?"

"Jake paid me $50,000 to embezzle funds from the company, but he also promised to split whatever I could siphon from the accounts, which turned out to be just under $6 million. And I know where most of that money is, I just can't access it."

"Then why leave now?"

"What do you mean?"

"If you're determined to get your $3 million, why leave now? Why not see it through to the end?"

"I did my part. I located Jake. It's Vinny's job to get the money."

"You're splitting $6 million with Vinny the *Prick*?"

"Yeah. But only because Jake left me no options."

"You said you located Jake. How? Did Taggart tell you where he's hiding?"

"I can't talk to you about that."

"Vinny will *kill* Jake!"

"No he won't. That's why I called *him* instead of Rocco, 'cause Rocco would *definitely* kill him if he found out Jake stole the money. But Vinny and Jake will come to an agreement without resorting to violence because Jake has millions squirreled away in other countries. He can pay Vinny the six million and still have enough left over to retire wealthy."

"What are the odds Vinny will give you half the money?"

"Zero. But I think he'll cough up at least 10%, which is more than I'll ever get from Jake."

"You know what I'm thinking? If we pool our money, we'll have enough! The six hundred thousand from Vinny, your fifty, the twenty thousand from the hospital, *my* million...wouldn't that be enough to start a lab in Thailand?"

"Bobby, I'll say it again: Jake didn't set aside a million dollars for you. Call the contact guy. You'll see."

"Okay. But don't throw your phone away. I want to be able to call you with the good news."

"Fine. I'll keep the phone, but don't call me before nine a.m. I'm exhausted."

Daisy hangs up and continues driving another hour through the dark night. As she approaches Jackson, her phone directs her to the nearest luxury hotel. When her screen lights up with the results, she lowers her expectations from clean and safe to cheap and available.

Now, in her room, she wastes little time getting to bed. She turns her phone off so Bobby won't wake her in the middle of a much-needed sleep.

At ten a.m., she gets up, pees, brushes her teeth, showers, and checks her messages. Not surprisingly, Bobby called her twice and left messages both times. She puts her phone on speaker, plays the first message, hears Bobby's excited voice say, "Happy St. Patrick's Day!"

She waits for the rest of the message, then checks the phone.

That was the entire message.

She frowns, plays the second message: "I've got news, Sleepyhead. Call me back!"

She turns on the television, wondering, *why do I care what happens to this guy?* She flips the stations till she gets to the news, and watches till her phone rings.

It's Bobby.

She puts the TV on mute and accepts the call: "Hey, Bobby. I just got up. So, what happened?"

"I called the contact guy."

"And?"

"He wired me the money!"

Daisy laughs. "Good for you, Bobby. That's great. Really, I'm happy for you."

"I want to share it with you, fifty-fifty."

"Stop."

"I'm serious. I want us to be together."

She nearly says something rude, but catches herself. A half-million dollars added to the $600,000 she expects to get from Vinny—if not more—is nothing to sneeze at. But could she live with herself, knowing what Bobby expects in return?

No.

Except that, how bad would it be to give him a try? He's super cute, he adores her, and he'd almost certainly treat her like a princess.

Bobby's voice interrupts her thoughts: "What do you say, Beautiful?"

She wants to say *Money won't buy my affection*, but what comes out of her mouth is: "You'd have to stop telling jokes."

"All jokes or just Confucius?"

She smiles to herself. Then says, "All jokes."

"Done."

"Bobby, you're sweet. But—"

"No. Don't say it. Let me speak first: I know it's too soon. I know it makes no sense...but I want you to trust my intuition. You're out of my league right now, but I can become a better man. And more importantly, I *want* to. So here's what I'm going to do: I'm going to wire $500,000 to your account right now, no strings attached...if you'll have dinner with me."

"That's a string right there."

"It's a thread, at most."

"That sounded a lot like a joke."

"It was. But it's okay, because we're not together yet. What do you say? Will you give me your checking account information?"

She thinks a long time before saying...

Chapter 36

"YES."

After giving Bobby the name and address of her bank, and the account and routing numbers, he asks, "Which name is on this account?"

It's too much: Daisy has to laugh. She's known him exactly 24 hours. Yesterday morning a hospital paid him eleven bucks to be anally probed by a dozen med students. Money was tight, but he didn't hesitate to offer her lunch and, shortly thereafter, half his religious artifacts business. Last night he became an instant millionaire, and his first thought was to share not only his fortune with her, but the rest of his life, as well. She said no, but he refused to give up on her. And now, insanely, he's offering her $500,000 to join him for dinner, while having not the first clue what her name is. Or at least the name she's currently using.

When he asked for her account information, Daisy knew he wouldn't care. She could have told him her new name, but why complicate things? He knows her as Daisy, and so that's the account information she gave him.

Thirty minutes later he calls to say the money's in her account, and asks if she has a choice of restaurants.

"You seriously wired a half-million dollars into my account?"

"I did. Call your bank. You'll see."

"You're crazy, you know that?"

"Yes."

"Why would you *do* that?"

"Like I said, I have a good feeling about us. Where are you? I'll come to you, so you won't have to drive."

"Jackson, Mississippi."

"I can be there in less than five hours."

"Bobby?"

"Yeah?"

"We're rich now. We can fly to dinner wherever we want."

"Do you have a place in mind?"

She was about to say Brooklyn, in the old family pizza parlor where she'd make him a custom pie that would knock his socks off. But they can't go there. Vinny bought the store from her dad and it's frequented by wiseguys who can't be trusted. One of Vinny's guys might tell one of Rocco's guys he saw Leah Shea—Jake's former bookkeeper—with Jake's brother Bobby. So she says, "You know what? Maybe we should save our money in case you talk me into doing something insane, like going to Thailand and starting a pharmaceutical company. But you don't have to drive all the way here. I'm glad to meet you half way."

"Don't be silly," Bobby says. "I *want* to come to Jackson. It's not safe here, and I'd rather be wherever you are. Plus, I assume you've already got a hotel room, right?"

"I thought you said the money came with no strings attached."

"I did. But...I mean, last night you were gonna go all the way for free!"

"Bobby?"

"Yeah?"

"That could happen tonight, too. But if it does, it won't be because you gave me money. Do you understand what I'm trying to say?"

"You're not a whore?"

"That's right."

"I already knew that. So anyway, want me to pick you up wherever you're staying, or would you rather meet at the restaurant?"

"The restaurant. At seven."

"See you then. But I'm anxious to get on the road. Can you pick a place and text me the name and address?"

"Of course. But if you leave now, you'll be too early. You'd have to sit around for hours before dinner."

"That's fine. I'll check into a hotel, get some rest, watch a little TV, take a shower..."

"Okay then. I'll come up with a nice place and text you before seven. Drive safely."

After hanging up, Daisy takes some time to evaluate the man who just gave her half his fortune for the chance to win her over. Could there possibly be a more generous guy on the planet? And if so, what are the chances she'd meet such a man and he'd fall in love with her the way Bobby has? Though she's known him a day, she has no doubt he means every word he said. He'd be faithful, devoted, and he'd continue to love her no matter what the future holds, which makes him unique among the men she's dated. But is he the sort of man with whom she could fall in love?

She ticks the items off her checklist.

Is he smart?

She winces. Ouch.

Well respected?

No.

Wealthy?

Yes. For now, at least. But he's gullible, easily manipulated, and doesn't respect the value of money, which means he's likely to lose it quickly.

Is he handsome?

Yes! Put an X in *that* box for sure!

Sexy?

Absolutely! Another X.

Is he classy?

Uh...no.

Funny?

No. Well, he tries. But...no. Not to her, anyway.

Is he ambitious?

Not really. But he's a dreamer. And a romantic. And those are good qualities, right?

Well, they *can* be.

Is he interesting?

Yes! He's definitely interesting. She pauses. Maybe not *consistently* interesting, but she'll give him the benefit of the doubt.

Is he good with kids?

Almost certainly, based on the fact that Cindy certainly likes him! ...But does she *want* kids?

No. She wants the freedom to do her research.

Is he honest?

Of course! Wait. *Is* he?

She calls her bank. Asks if the wire transfer has taken place. Her call gets transferred to an account executive named Lucinda Lincoln, who says:

Chapter 37

"PLEASE: CALL ME Lucy. And yes, we're showing $500,000 has been wired to your account. We're very happy to have you as a customer, and I hope you'll give me the opportunity to introduce you to our estate planning committee in the near future."

"Sadly, I'll need you to wire the money to another account before 2 p.m. today."

Lucy says, "That's not possible. International funds can't be accessed for at least three business days."

Daisy asks why and gets a banking lecture she doesn't understand, since she was under the impression that Bobby's bank, Cane River Bank & Trust, wired the funds a scant 30 minutes after receiving them. Which is how she learned the money came from Geneva, Switzerland, not Bobby's bank.

Daisy thanks her for the information, then provides the wiring instructions for whenever the funds become available.

"Oh dear," Lucy says.

"What now?"

"We can't wire this amount of money to an offshore business account in the Bahamas."

"Why not?"

"We have to notify the IRS of any transaction of $10,000 or higher."

"Yes, of course," Daisy says. "I'm okay with that."

"You may want to re-think that, since Nassau's a well-known tax haven, and the new administration is cracking down on transactions that involve moving money outside the United States. They're going to want details regarding the source of your funds."

"You're joking."

"I'm sorry. Plus, you'll have to file Form 8300 within 15 days for all amounts over $10,000. As for wiring half a *million* to the Bahamas? That's a major transaction. You don't have to answer, but I wonder if you happen to own the business you're planning to wire the money to?"

"I'll say yes, hypothetically."

"Have you filed an FFBAR with the Bahamian government?"

"What's that?"

"Form TDF 90-22.1."

"Oh. Thanks for clearing that up for me."

Lucy laughs. "It's a report you have to file if you have a financial account in a foreign country with a value exceeding $10,000 at any time during the calendar year. Otherwise you could be in deep you-know-what."

"Fine. Forget about wiring the money. How long before I can get a certified check for the entire sum?"

"Three business days."

"Thank you. I'll see you on Friday."

"Ms. Pepper? I really think you and I should meet before you attempt to access the funds. It can be very difficult to navigate the banking laws and regulations, not to mention the recent guidelines. There are a number of pitfalls I can help you avoid." She pauses, then lowers her voice and says, "I'd welcome the opportunity to take you to lunch and *personally* walk you through the options, if you understand what I'm proposing."

"Could any of these options be considered loopholes?"

"Yes. And I can think of three that might solve your problems."

"Can I assume this would be a private discussion that will involve my paying a fee to you and not the bank?"

"Yes indeed. But I'm sure you'll find my fee quite reasonable, given the possible repercussions for attempting to move large sums of money from questionable sources out of the country."

"In that case, I'll absolutely meet you for lunch on Friday! Thank you, Lucy!"

"My pleasure."

After ending the call, Daisy turns on the TV and learns the Irish Prime Minister and his entourage have been insulted by not only the President, but the Vice President, and Speaker of the House, as well.

Daisy's not a political person. In fact, she didn't even vote in the recent election. But everything about this administration makes her cringe. Can it really be true the VP said "Top of the Morning!" to the Irish visitors? That's like holding up a hand and saying "How" to an American Indian. Then the President had great difficulty reading what he claimed was one of his favorite Irish proverbs, which turned out to be a poem, not a proverb, written by a Nigerian, not an Irishman! Then the Speaker of the House gave a toast with a non-foaming glass of beer, apparently unaware the Irish consume their beer with a huge head of foam and consider anything less to be an insult. To make matters worse, he spoke of how playing golf—which even *Daisy* knows was invented in Scotland, not Ireland—was as close to *royalty* as we get in the USA! Because if there's one thing the Irish *love*, it's *royalty*, right?

"*Jesus!*" she shouts at the TV. "These are our *allies*! Do your fucking homework, people!"

Bobby thinks she was a Hillary supporter.

She's wasn't. If given the chance, she would have voted for Kasich, a Republican.

But at least Hillary did her homework.

Meanwhile, Bobby's an "Oh hell, yeah!" Trump supporter, which means their political views—at least with respect to women—are hopelessly incompatible. Not that she cares that much about politics. Daisy takes a minute to think about the few things she and Bobby have in common and the many things they don't. People always say opposites attract. But do they stay together?

She wonders.

Then her phone rings.

It's Vinny.

"Hello?" she says.

"We got him!"

"You got Jake?"

"Yeah. Him and his girlfriend."

Daisy pauses. She doesn't want to tell Vinny that Jake's girlfriend is in the hospital. No sense exposing Eileen to these mobsters. "What makes you think she's his girlfriend?"

"They were fuckin' when my guys got there. Are you jealous?"

"No."

"Good."

Daisy can't believe Jake's been fucking her, and Eileen, and now someone else while Eileen's in the hospital. Still, she hears her voice ask, "Is she cute?"

"I didn't ask. But next time we talk? I'll have that answer for you. Not that I like the question, 'cause I don't. It tells me you still got a thing for him. You don't need that bastard. You got me now, understand?"

"Yeah."

"Then act like it."

Daisy ends the call and springs into action. She surfs the Internet, exchanges some emails, makes some calls, meets some people. Eventually, she makes a reservation at Percola's Restaurant for two people at 7 o'clock, and texts the information to Bobby.

He texts back: *Thanks. I was beginning to get worried! I'm in Jackson. Can't wait to see you!*

Daisy wonders what the chances are that he'd choose the same motel she did. She peers out the window and checks the parking lot carefully. His car's not there.

Just to be sure, she texts him back, asks where he's staying, and he confirms he's downtown, which is nearly six miles away.

She removes some items from her suitcase, takes them to the bathroom, stares at herself in the mirror, and sighs.

Time to change her look.

Chapter 38

AT 6:55 P.M., BOBBY enters the restaurant and looks around. Only six people in the foyer, none of them Daisy, so he heads to the bar.

She's not there, either.

He checks his watch, then approaches the hostess, a stunning young lady with hypnotic, pyrite-colored eyes and jet-black hair parted down the middle. "Cujo, party of two," he says.

She looks at him. "Are you okay?"

"You should see the other guy."

"If I did, I'd slap him. Hard!"

Bobby smiles. "I wish you'd been there. I could've used the help."

"Are you in pain?"

"Not so much. It was a lot worse yesterday."

"Well, I hope you enjoy your dinner."

He winks. "I'm already enjoying it."

They stare at each other a moment, then she leans over to check the reservation book, and Bobby does his best to avoid looking down her blouse, but the angle's so perfect he decides if God didn't want him seeing her boobs He would have made them less inviting. She catches him looking, which embarrasses him more than her, a fact made obvious by the smile she offers…and the way she looks around, lowers her voice and says, "I'm Taylor." And the way she removes one of the business cards from the stack on the front desk, turns it over, writes her digits on the back, hands it to him and says, "I broke up with my boyfriend last night. No promises, but if that sounds like an opportunity to you, I get off at eleven."

Before Bobby can speak, the second hostess returns to the desk, eager for her next assignment. Taylor's voice turns professional: "Mr. Cujo, your guest arrived early and asked to be seated. Would you care to join her now?"

"Please."

"Marie will escort you to Table 22," she says, flashing a dazzling smile that—if not for Daisy's presence in his life—would fry his brain circuits. As Marie leads him through the maze of tables in the dining area, Taylor's smile stays with him, and he can't help but remember what Jake said about romance being overrated. Yes, his marriage to Eileen was a bigger disaster than the '71 Ford Pinto. But here he is again, consumed by romantic yearning, working his ass off to win Daisy's heart: Daisy, who's aloof, opinionated, with tons of baggage (both mental and dangerous), who's probably never going to love him anyway. Meanwhile, in this very restaurant, Taylor—a forthright young lady with exemplary tits and epic eyes—is clearly into him, and appears to be his for the taking.

No need to ask himself what Jake would do!

He turns to look at Taylor, hoping to see her pyrite eyes still on him, but she's focused on the line of customers in the entryway, just as she should be.

When Marie stops and gestures to the table, Bobby says, "I think there's been a mistake."

He looks around at the nearby tables for Daisy, but doesn't see her. What he *does* see in the seat meant for Daisy is a blonde, approximately twenty-two years of age, who's smiling at him, and pushing a gift-wrapped package toward the empty chair. The blonde says, "Bobby? Please sit. I have some information about Daisy."

"Who are *you*?"

Marie says, "Is everything alright?"

Bobby nods, tentatively sits, and watches Marie as she glides back to the front desk. He continues staring as Marie and Taylor exchange words, and now Taylor's looking at him to see if he's okay, but the young lady at his table breaks his concentration, saying, "If I were your date, I'd find your behavior exceptionally rude."

Without bothering to face her, Bobby says, "I'm looking for Daisy."

"Well, I can tell you this much: she's not surgically attached to Marie's ass."

Now Bobby turns. The young lady pushes the gift closer to him. Bobby stares at it a moment, then looks up and says, "I'm sorry. *Who are you?*"

"You can't tell the resemblance?"

"What are you talking about?"

"I'm Julie: the missing sister."

Chapter 39

BOBBY'S JAW DROPS. "That's bullshit!"

The young lady giggles. "You're right. That *is* bullshit. I was kidding. Daisy told me to say that."

Bobby stares at the package and frowns, unable to hide his disappointment. "What else did she say?"

"Not much. She asked me to meet you, give you this gift, and entertain you for an hour."

Bobby's face brightens. "She's been delayed?"

"I don't know. She just asked if I'd keep you company for an hour."

"Where did you meet her?"

"Coffee shop."

"Today? Just out of the blue?"

"No. Ever heard of ItsJustCoffee.co?"

"Not really."

"It's a no-pressure dating site. Instead of tying up an entire evening, or lunch, you just agree to have coffee. Then, if you like each other, you can take it from there."

"You met her for coffee?"

"Yes."

"Why would you want to meet Daisy for coffee? Are you gay?"

The young lady's eyes go huge. "*Excuse* me? That is literally the most intellectually-challenged, politically incorrect, intolerant, homophobic question I've ever been asked. You're quite rude, aren't you?" She pauses. "Are you even aware that you questioned my sexual orientation before asking my name?"

He holds up both hands as if surrendering. "Look, I didn't mean to come across rude."

"Perhaps you just can't help yourself."

He runs his hand through his hair before saying, "Here's the thing: I drove a long way to see Daisy tonight, and your presence caught me by surprise. I know I've been rude, and I'm sorry. But I'm horribly disappointed she didn't show up, and I'm trying to get a handle on who you are and why you're here. Did she *pay* you to be here?"

"Yes. And while I accept your apology, I feel obligated to say she made you sound a lot nicer at the coffee shop today."

"I'm glad to hear that. How much did she pay you?"

"Why does that matter?"

He shrugs.

She goes quiet and matches his mood for a short time. But since it's not her nature to be negative, she takes a deep breath, extends her hand, and puts as much cheer in her voice as possible, saying: "How about we start over. Pretend we just met! Hi, I'm Abby Dale!"

As he stares at her hand he suddenly confronts the possibility Daisy isn't coming at all, and may have paid this young lady to be his dinner date. For her part, Abby can't believe he's refusing to shake her hand. Stunned by his rudeness, she angrily withdraws her hand, places it in her lap and mutters, "And you must be Prince Charming."

Bobby doesn't pick up on her sarcasm. He's too busy staring at the Hostess Desk, which prompts Abby to say, "*Really*, Bobby?"

He waits till he's certain there are no customers in the foyer. Then stands and says, "Give me a sec. I'll be right back."

"Suit yourself," she says, fighting not to add the word *Asshole*.

Bobby strides forcefully through the dining area. Taylor sees him coming and rewards him with another of her patented smiles. But as he gets closer, she can see that he's glaring. As her smile rapidly fades, she asks, "Is everything okay?"

"How much?" he barks.

"Excuse me?"

"How much did she pay you to flirt with me?"

Taylor's eyes go wide. She looks around nervously, and whispers with urgency: "Please. Keep your voice down."

Bobby lowers his voice, but not nearly enough. "What was the end game? *Sex*? Are you some kind of *hooker*?"

She slaps him full force. Horrified, Marie rushes to get help. By the time she returns with the manager, Taylor's crying, and Bobby's deep into his apology. He extends it to the manager, and she asks Taylor what happened. Taylor says, "It was just a misunderstanding."

The manager eyes Bobby carefully. "Did you touch her?"

"No Ma'am. I mean, I slapped me, but I didn't...um..."

She turns to Taylor, who says, "It's true. There was no sexual assault."

"Then what happened?"

She looks at Bobby and says, "He...I mean...I..." she starts to cry again.

The manager says, "The bottom line is you slapped one of our customers. That can't be tolerated."

Bobby says, "I deserved it. I made a vulgar remark. I'm...I don't know why I said it. I'm not myself today. I'm truly sorry. But Taylor did the right thing. Please don't punish her for it."

Now a tall, muscular waiter sidles up beside Taylor, assumes a protective stance, and shows Bobby a malevolent stare. The manager says, "This doesn't concern you, Jeff. Go back to your station." Jeff pauses, looks at Taylor, and doesn't leave until she nods it's okay.

The manager says, "With all due respect, Sir, it's not your job to discipline my employees. And whatever you said to her, whatever the reason, doesn't justify her assaulting a customer. Taylor? You're fired. Collect your personal items and leave the property immediately."

Taylor stares at her in total shock, as if she can't believe what she's hearing.

The manager grabs some tissues from a box behind the desk, hands them to Taylor and says, "Don't make a scene, or you'll get a lousy reference."

Taylor closes her eyes a moment, sets her jaw, and collects her composure. She takes a deep breath, wipes her face, then, with great dignity, strides purposefully toward the kitchen with Jeff the waiter following close behind.

The manager's eyes narrow. "Your dinner will of course be complimentary tonight. Please enjoy the rest of your evening." She turns to leave.

Bobby says, "Wait. I don't want you to comp my dinner. This whole thing was my fault. There must be *something* I can do to make you reconsider."

"Sorry, but assaulting customers is a clear violation of the employee handbook." She starts to leave again, then turns and says, "You know what *really* sucks? Taylor didn't deserve this. Whatever you felt compelled to say to her, I hope it was worth it, because I'm going to miss her. She's one of my best employees. She'll be hard to replace."

"Please?"

"Not going to happen. Is there anything else you require to make your dining experience pleasurable tonight?"

Bobby hangs his head.

"Then I suggest you go back to your table and put this unfortunate incident behind you." She leaves, and Bobby immediately calls the number Taylor gave him. When her phone goes to voicemail he says: "*It's me, Bobby Cujo. I'm so sorry about what happened just now. Please give me a chance to make it up to you. At least financially, if nothing else. You can call me at this number any time. And I hope you will.*"

Bobby skulks back to his table.

Abby says, "Bad day just got worse?"

"You could say that."

"Maybe you should open the gift."

"No need. I already know what it is."

"Do you also know what the note says?"

He looks up with interest. "There's a note?"

"I would assume so."

"Why?"

Abby shrugs. "I don't claim to be an official spokesperson for my gender, but I can tell you with great confidence that women rarely wrap gifts without enclosing a note."

Bobby rips the paper off, opens the box, and places the Moon Pie, wrapped in tissue paper, on the table. He searches the box for a note. Then says, "Got any other great ideas?"

"I would have put it in the tissue paper."

He removes the tissue paper from the Moon Pie, and...Abby's right: there's a note. He opens it and reads:

Chapter 40

BOBBY, AS YOU know by now, I stood you up. You're probably pissed you drove all those miles for nothing, but as it turned out, leaving Louisiana may have saved your life.

Vinny called. He's got Jake, and they're working out a financial arrangement for the six million even as you're reading these words. But what we didn't know, Rocco put out a hit on you. As a favor to me, Vinny talked him into canceling it, but these favors don't come cheap, and so I had to give Rocco half my share (he thinks there's only $3 million total). To put it another way, if Vinny comes through, he'll get three million, and Rocco and I will split the other three. But in the end, if Vinny decides to shaft me, what recourse do I have?

The good news is you won't have to flee the country! You'll be safe the minute Rocco gets his cash, but until then I strongly recommend you stay in Jackson—or at least out of Louisiana—for about a week, since it could take several business days before Rocco can access the cash.

Bobby, I want you to know I thought long and hard about sharing a life with you. But surely you can see we're just too different to be more than friends, or a short fling. And I know that's not what you're seeking. So, I have a question for you:

How do you like Abby so far? Personally, I think she's a doll. She's cute, smart, upbeat, and—brace yourself—I think she might be normal! I know you gravitate to the hot crazies, but the cute normals are the key to a man's happiness, so I hope you'll give Abby a chance. Now before you start acting weird, let me assure you, I didn't pay her to go out with you. I only paid her to meet you, give you the Moon Pie, and spend an hour with you to see if there's a connection. And I hope there is!

Be safe, Bobby.

Love,

Daisy

PS: I know the money you wired to my account was given in love, so I intend to keep it and put it to good use.

Chapter 41

"EITHER IT'S A long letter or you're a slow reader," Abby says, cheerfully.

"Both."

He looks at her through different eyes.

"Well, hello!" she says, brightly. "*There* you are! *Finally!*"

Upset as he is, he almost laughs out loud. Daisy's right: Abby's exactly the type of woman his mother would have picked for him: she's prettier than attractive, less threatening than gorgeous, with a cuteness factor that's through the roof. She's perky, intelligent, forgiving, and genuinely nice.

Great wife material, for certain.

But after paying Daisy a half-million dollars to have dinner with him, and getting stood up, he's not in the mood to start a new relationship.

He wants to get laid.

"I'm sorry," he says. "I know Daisy had high hopes that we'd meet and hit it off, but—"

Abby's face falls. "It's okay," she says. "I understand. Truly I do." But her look says she's taking it personally, as if she failed to measure up. As she pushes her chair back and reaches for her purse Bobby says, "Please hear me out. You've been...amazing, and I've been a total jerk."

She stands. "It's okay, Bobby. Wasn't meant to be, that's all." She offers a sad smile. "Story of my life."

Bobby says, "I was going to ask Daisy to marry me tonight."

Her jaw drops. "I had no idea. That's...so sad! No wonder you were acting like—um...I mean—"

He looks up and smiles. "Like an asshole?"

She smiles, sits back down. "Let me put a title on it: you like me, but the timing's bad."

"Exactly."

She puts her hand on his. "You shouldn't be alone tonight. How about we order dinner: it'll be my treat."

He laughs. "Could you possibly be any nicer?"

Abby smiles at the compliment and fights the urge to say something self-deprecating in response. They stare into each other's eyes, contemplating the possibilities: she wonders if this is the man she'll marry someday, and he wonders if this is the woman he'll fuck tonight.

Bobby's phone rings, shattering the mood.

"Hello?"

"It's me, Taylor."

Jumping to his feet, Bobby says, "Hang on a sec!" He covers the phone and whispers to Abby: "I need to take this. I'll be right back."

She nods, watches him hurry away so preoccupied with his call that he bumps the table of a pale young lady who's dining alone, wearing a dilapidated dress and a cancer kerchief to cover her shaved head. Though he spills her water glass, he doesn't stop to offer help. Thankfully, a waiter rushes to her aid, but in Abby's eyes, common decency would compel Bobby to...at the very least...

She sighs.

She's seen and heard enough. Specifically, she heard a woman's voice on the phone and noted Bobby's reaction to it. As she watches him rush through the restaurant lobby and into the men's room so he can take his call in private, she stands, loops her purse over her shoulder, and walks out the door.

Moments later the pale young lady with the cancer kerchief removes a piece of paper from her purse, writes down a name and phone number, and places it on the table beside the Moon Pie. Then she goes back to her seat and finishes her entrée.

Ten minutes later, Bobby returns to an empty table. It's for the best, he decides, having already arranged a date with the hot young Taylor that promises mega fireworks. He places some money on the table, reaches for the Moon Pie, and sees the note. He scoops it up, reads it, and smiles. Abby left her name and number. He pockets it, and heads for the door.

The young lady in the cancer kerchief answers her phone. The voice on the other end says, "It's Taylor. The date's on, but I just want to be 100% clear on the money situation."

"You get $10,000 for sleeping with him," Daisy says, adjusting her kerchief, and $2,000 for every night you go out with him over the next seven days."

Taylor says, "I appreciate the thousand you paid me to flirt, but this goes way beyond that. No offense, but I've never met you before today, and the details of how you found me are awfully sketchy."

"You're listed on three escort services."

"Right. But how did you know I was hostessing at Percola's?"

"I didn't. But the restaurant didn't matter. Like I said this afternoon, I posted a query with the local escort community for a waitress, and your name came up."

"But I'm a hostess."

"Even better."

"The reason it's sketchy: I don't know any of the other escorts in town, and my clients have no idea where I work."

"Surely you don't believe that! Jackson's a small town, and you're gorgeous. If Melania Trump showed up at a pot luck she wouldn't get more attention than you."

"Well, that's nice of you to say, but the reason I'm calling, I'd like half the payment up front. In cash. Before my date tonight."

"What if he says no to sleeping with you?"

Taylor laughs. "You're joking, right?"

"Good point. I don't know what came over me to pose the question in the first place. More to the point, I've got enough cash to accommodate your request. Are you still here?"

"I'm in the parking lot. But the date's in thirty minutes."

"Okay. I'm walking out now."

Taylor says, "Did you see my big scene? He got me fired tonight."

"I *did*. You're a natural."

"I'm in the black Celica."

"I see you."

Daisy pays her, and Taylor says, "Just so you know, he wants to give me something to make up for getting me fired. I assume that's okay with you."

"Of course. Within reason. Just remember he's a nice guy. I wouldn't want you to take advantage of him."

"I'm grateful, not greedy."

"I hope that's true."

"You'll pay me the balance tomorrow morning?"

"Of course. Assuming you earn it."

"I always do. Where and when?"

"How about right here, at ten."

"I'll be here. By the way, is there anything I need to know about this guy?"

"Like what?"

"Is he a hitter? A biter? Is he into domination? Submission? Bondage? Does he have anger issues? Mommy issues? Gender issues? Can he get it up? Does he expect—"

Daisy interrupts her: "I think he's pretty normal, except for penis size."

"Small or big?"

"Big."

Taylor frowns. "Porn star big or Guinness World Record big?"

Daisy laughs. "I forgot who I was talking to. You'll be fine."

Chapter 42

TWO BLOCKS FROM the bar in downtown Jackson, at the stop light, Bobby checks his teeth in the mirror. Pissed as he is, he can't help but grin at his reflection while saying, "You've still got it, Cujo!" He wonders how many guys in the world could have scored a date with a gorgeous girl like Taylor after getting her fired.

"You're one of a kind, Cujo," he says.

Two hours later, while being fucked, Taylor says, "*What* did you just say?"

"Nothing."

But he *had* said something. His exact words were: "Fuck you, Daisy!"

Fortunately, Taylor let it slide. Five minutes later, after coaxing the last drop of fluid from his penis, she slides out from under him and Bobby, still breathing heavily, tells her: "That was the best sex of my life."

"Thank you, Bobby. It was great for me, too."

He props himself up on an elbow and says, "You're the most beautiful woman I've ever met in my whole life."

She kisses his cheek. "That is so sweet! Thank you!"

"It's true. I've got a really good feeling about you, Taylor. Crazy as this might sound, I think this was meant to happen."

She looks into his eyes and purrs, "I think so, too."

At that exact moment, less than six miles away, a large, powerful man is beating the shit out of Daisy Pepper in her hotel room.

Chapter 43

THE MAN FOLLOWED Daisy from the restaurant parking lot to her hotel, then caught the same elevator, held the door in check with his arm and let her exit first. He followed, and kept walking past her when she placed her magnetic key card over the door lock. When it clicked, he pivoted, and moved quickly. When she pushed the door open he was right behind her. Before she realized what was happening, he punched the back of her head, knocking her face down onto the floor. Then he kicked her legs out of the way, closed the door behind him and as she rolled over to face him he punched her jaw three times.

Overkill, since the first blow rendered her unconscious.

When she came to, the world was blurry. The clothes from her suitcase were strewn all over the floor and he was sitting on the king bed, going through the dumped contents of her purse. She must have made a sound just now because he's looking at her, saying, "Where's the rest of it?"

He's talking about the money. He's already got about four thousand, but assumes there's more.

He's right.

It's in the glove box of her rental car.

And in the console.

But the bulk of it—nearly thirty grand—is in the wheel well, under the spare tire. She hopes if worse comes to worse and she has to tell him about the cash in the car, he'll think he's got it all, and won't check the trunk. Because that's where she also hid her new ID and two burner phones.

"I asked you a question, Cancer Girl," he says.

She gets her swollen mouth to say, "Glove compartment."

"These the keys?" he asks, holding them up.

"Yes."

"What's this?"

She tries to focus.

"There's two of 'em," he says.

No need to focus. He's referring to the remaining vials of snake venom.

"Cancer meds," she says.

"What kind?"

She rubs her jaw. How can the simple act of speaking be so painful?

"Interferon-beta," she says. "In liquid form."

"That makes it work faster?"

"Yes."

"What's it do, give you energy?"

"Yes."

"Good. If you're nice, I might give you some. Would you like that?"

When she fails to answer, he says, "Speaking of giving you some, maybe I'll fuck you, too. How does *that* sound?"

Not good, she thinks. Aside from her natural aversion to being raped, her Daisy Pepper ID is currently located in her panties for a very good reason: she recognized this guy the moment he entered the elevator.

He's a waiter.

Specifically, he's Jeff, the waiter from Percola's, who followed Taylor to the kitchen after she slapped Bobby and got fired. Which means he's either her boyfriend, her pimp, or both. But whatever their relationship, it's clear that Taylor set her up. When he entered the elevator, he noticed the lit button indicating the third floor and said, "Me too." Then, as if noticing her shaved head for the first time, said, "I feel for you. Cancer's a bitch."

Daisy almost said, "I know you!" but held back. Something about him wasn't right. For one thing, his presence in the elevator: why wasn't he working at Percola's? Did he quit after Taylor got fired? If so, what was he doing at her hotel? He's locally employed, so she doubts he's staying at the hotel. And what were the chances they'd be on the same floor?

Following her intuition, Daisy backed up in the elevator, keeping him in front of her while she slipped her Daisy Pepper ID into the back of her jeans, under her panties. Since it's the only way she can access the $500,000 Bobby wired to her account in Nashville, it made sense to protect it at all costs. When the elevator stopped at her floor, she waited for him to leave first, but he held the door open, so she walked straight to her room, paused, and waited till he kept going. Then she opened the door as quickly as possible, but not quickly enough, and now he's threatening to rape her.

Daisy hates her cancer-patient disguise. She knows it takes a low person to fake an illness, but she's in hiding, and since he's totally buying it, the disguise is serving her well. Thinking she's far weaker than she is, he might let his guard down. And speaking of low, what kind of scumbag would beat, rob, and rape a cancer patient?

This guy would, and proves it by saying: "Get naked. Jeans first. And be grateful I didn't break your nose. I could have, you know."

She moves slowly, feigning weakness. Starts with her belt, then slowly slides her zipper down, and...

His phone rings.

His natural impulse is to turn his head and whisper into his phone, and Daisy takes that opportunity to locate her ID and stuff it in the pocket of a pair of pants he already searched. When he turns his attention back to her and motions her to move faster, she works her way into a sitting position and removes her shoes and jeans. Jeff suddenly stands and grabs the jeans and searches through them with one hand while holding the phone with his other. When he sits back down on the bed she hears him say, "Yeah. Little over four grand, but there's more in the car." He's quiet a minute, listening. Then says, "I'll leave when I'm damn good and ready." He pauses again, then says, "Oh really? *You're* threatening *me?* I'll fuck whoever I want. It's not like you weren't fucking just now!" Pause. "Yeah, that's right: a cancer patient!" Pause. "Well, fuck you, too!"

He clicks the phone off and says, "Hurry up. I want you naked, on the bed. *Now!*" When Daisy's top comes off, he licks his lips and sweeps the contents of her purse onto the floor to make room for her on the bed.

"Let's see the rest," he says, with great enthusiasm.

Daisy removes her bra and says, "If you give me a dose of the interferon and wait two minutes you'll have a much better time."

"Nice try, but I don't give a shit if you're any good in bed. You can lie there like you're dead, for all I care."

She says, "Have it your way, but any pressure on my abdomen could cause me to shit myself."

"Whoa. I'm not into that." He searches the floor with his eyes, then picks up one of the vials. "This keeps you from *shitting* yourself?"

She nods.

"Fine. But I'm not gonna hand it to you, 'cause you could throw it at me and put my eye out."

He opens the lid and says, "Come here, and I'll pour it down your throat."

She picks up one of her shoes and hurls it at his face, and when he ducks to avoid it the venom spills onto his neck and chest, causing his body to immediately shut down. As he lies dying on the bed, lungs constricting, gasping for breath, Daisy washes her face, gets dressed, gathers her items, and places them back in her purse. She checks Jeff's pulse to make sure he's dead, then re-packs her suitcase and wipes all the surfaces with a wet towel, paying special attention to the droplets of blood he caused her to spill on the carpet. Then she gets in her car, drives north till she crosses the state line, and checks into a hotel in Memphis using her new ID. After consuming one of the pain pills she purloined from Bobby's stash, she reads the "fuck you" text Bobby sent her, which prompts her to text back: *Charming. I'm sure you enjoyed your evening of debauchery, but you know what they say: "Never fall in love with a hooker."* She adds a link to Taylor's escort page, then smashes the phone, tosses half the pieces in the parking lot dumpster and the rest in the gas station trash receptacle across the street, while filling her tank. Tomorrow she'll drive to Nashville and meet Lucy Lincoln, who, for a price, will share some ideas about how to transfer an obscene amount of money overseas without running afoul of the law.

Now, back in her hotel room, Daisy attempts to order room service, but finds the restaurant has closed for the night. She grabs one of her new burner phones, punches Vinny dePazzio's number in it, and texts: *Daisy's new phone number. Stand by for my call.*

She waits two minutes, then calls. He answers, and right away she knows there's a problem.

Chapter 44

"WE GOT THE wrong guy," Vinny says.

"What do you mean?"

"You know Jake's driver?"

"Charley?"

"Yeah."

"What about him?"

"He's dead. So anyway, the big tent in the woods ain't Jake's. I mean, he bought it and put it there, but that ain't where he's hidin'."

"How do you know?"

"My guys followed Charley there and it turns out Jake sold the tent to some guy from Gonzales who uses it for a fuck shack."

"That can't be true."

"It is, though. And by the way, it's only about thirty minutes from downtown Gonzales, so it wouldn't make sense for Jake to hide there, anyway. But yeah, accordin' to Charley he used it two nights ago to meet Bobby. Then he paid Charley to drive there twice a day to see if anyone was followin' him. Jake's got cameras in the trees around the tent. My guys missed 'em at first."

Daisy shakes her head with disgust. Can anything else possibly go wrong?

"Here's what I don't understand," she says. "This morning you said you had Jake and you were working out the finances."

"Yeah. Because that's what my guys told me. They put a gun to Charley's head and made him take 'em to the tent. Found a man and woman inside. Based on what *you* said, we assumed it was Jake, so I called to tell you the good news. Then we found out he was just some rich guy, fuckin' another man's wife."

"Why didn't you call to tell me?"

"We kept thinkin' it was Jake, makin' up excuses, so I told the guys to do whatever it took to get to the truth. By the time they were done, the man and woman were as dead as Charley, and their story never changed."

"Did anyone say where Jake was?"

"Trust me, they didn't know."

"Shit!"

"Yeah. That's how I feel, too."

"What about Rocco? You got him to call off the hit on Bobby, right?"

"Yeah, but it's on again. Any idea where he is?"

"No clue."

"Call him, see if he'll tell you."

"Why?"

"Rocco's payin' fifty grand. Tell me where he is, and I'll give you ten percent."

"I wouldn't do that to Bobby."

"You don't have a choice. I already told Rocco I had a lead on the guy. And you're it."

Chapter 45

DAISY COMES WITHIN an inch of hanging up on Vinny, then thinks better of it, realizing she needs more information.

"Did you ever find out why Rocco wants Bobby dead?"

"There's a rumor he killed two of Rocco's guys."

"I don't believe that!"

"Don't matter what you believe. When you comin' back?"

"Couple days."

"The pizza parlor ain't the same without you. Not to mention I miss you."

When she fails to comment, he says, "You miss me?"

"Not really."

He laughs. "God, you're a spitfire. I love that about you. Not to mention your fine ass!"

"That ass came with a price. We had a deal."

"We did. And you gave me some shit information, so that part's over."

"What do you mean?"

"The only shot we had at the money was you knowing about it in the first place, and your plan to use Bobby to find Jake. But you fucked that up, and now Rocco's got twenty guys searchin' the state. We'll never find him first. It's over."

"Does Rocco know about the embezzlement?"

"No."

"So he doesn't know we're looking for Jake."

"What's your point?"

"What if I can still find him?"

"You'd have to find him, hold him somewhere safe, get the money, then turn him over to Rocco."

"That's a death sentence for Jake."

"Why do *you* care? He ditched you, remember?"

How could she forget? While she was working her ass off trying to manipulate the company's cash without getting caught, Jake was hiding in a tent, fucking Bobby's wife. During that time, she quietly changed her name to Daisy Pepper, secured a passport, and when the day came, she dutifully flew to Bangkok and waited for his flight to arrive. When he wasn't on it, she texted him repeatedly, but got no answer. She waited all afternoon and evening, and after he failed to show on the last flight of the night, she got a cab and checked into the hotel she'd reserved for their first night together as a couple.

After two days with no word from Jake, she called the banking connection Jake gave her and was told he no longer worked there. Concerned, but still trusting Jake, she continued to follow the script: she posed for her new ID and passport, and picked it up two days later. She deviated from the plan by purchasing three vials of blue coral snake venom that she planned to use for experiments. But by the fifth day it was clear even to her that Jake wasn't coming. As her slow boil turned to fury, she called Vinny dePazzio, who'd bought her father's pizza parlor. After exchanging a few pleasantries, she said, "Want to share $3 million with me?"

He answered, "I'd rather have it all."

Daisy hung up on him, flew back to the States, went back to work making pizzas. Her second day of work, Vinny showed up. "Okay, you win," he said. "Tell me about the three million."

From there, it was game on: a plan was hatched, and Bobby was the key to its success.

Most of the many lies she told were off-the-cuff. There was no missing sister. No Joey Zorba. No ice pick in the chest that prompted a dying confession about Jake having a long-lost brother. Daisy already knew Jake had a brother because she dated him before his mob troubles began. Back then he delighted in describing his kid brother as "a total fuck up." She just didn't remember Bobby's name, or where he lived, or where he worked, but the Internet yielded the information she needed to track him down.

And so she did, and now his life's in danger.

Danger?

Let's be honest: Bobby's a dead man.

The smart thing to do is obvious: she should forget about Jake's money, move forward with her life, enjoy the half-million Bobby gave her, and let this whole Rocco thing play out. Rocco's goons will kill Bobby, and eventually they'll find Jake, and kill him, as well. In the meantime, Rocco will liquidate Jake's company and never learn about the embezzled funds. And if he *does* find out, he'll assume it was Jake, acting alone.

Her chances are decent: she won't have to leave the country because no one in America—not even Jake—knows her new identity. Which means she can access the money Bobby gave her, pick a place to live, and transfer the funds into an account under her new name, and start her new life.

Certain changes will have to be made: she'll have to cease contact with every person she knows. Her appearance will need to be altered dramatically. And she'll have to abandon her fascination with blue coral snakes, now that two men in two days have been killed by its venom in hotel rooms rented by a woman who looks exactly like Daisy did, before she shaved her head.

There's only one loose end:

Vinny knows she and Jake embezzled money from Jake's company. And that piece of information could be a bargaining chip for Vinny to use in future dealings with Rocco. If she keeps seeing Vinny, no problem: he'll keep her secret. But Bobby was right to call her a whore. She did, in fact, have sex with Vinny, who demanded she be his mistress in return for providing the muscle to force Jake to clean out his safe deposit boxes. No matter what happens to her in the future, that will always be the low point of her life. Just *thinking* about what she did with Vinny, hoping to get access to Jake's money, makes her want to vomit.

Bobby may have his faults, but he's a much better person than she is. And despite calling him names and standing him up and accepting his money, she realizes she has true feelings for him.

It sucks that he has to die.

On cue, Vinny says, "Where's Bobby Cujo?"

"I'm not sure."

"Last chance," he says.

Even as she says it she can't believe the words are coming out of her mouth: "Jackson, Mississippi."

"That's my girl. Where in Jackson?"

Chapter 46

DAISY HAS THREE phones left, and only two chargers. She pulls the charger out of the old Vinny phone and plugs it into the new one. Then calls Bobby, hears his phone ring twice, then gets a message that the call was refused.

***

210 miles away, in Jackson, Mississippi, Bobby's phone rang twice, and woke him up. He checked the number. Unable to recognize it, he rejected the call.

Seconds later, he gets a text from the same number:

Bobby, it's me, Daisy. This is life or death. I'm not kidding. Please take my call.

When she calls back, Taylor murmurs, "What time is it?"

Bobby tells her.

"Shit. I can't believe I fell asleep. Who's calling you?"

"I have no idea. I don't recognize the number."

"Then don't accept it."

"No problem." He rejects Daisy's call again.

Taylor reaches for the lamp on the night stand, turns it on, and climbs out of bed. As she puts on her panties and starts gathering her clothes, Bobby says, "I thought you were spending the night."

"Were you not paying attention earlier? I was waiting on a phone call that never came. Something's wrong."

Defensively, Bobby says, "I *did* pay attention: we made love, then you got up and took your phone to the bathroom and called someone, and sounded pissed. But when I asked you about it you said it wasn't important."

"Well, it was. I didn't want to ruin the mood, but it was my brother. They took my dad to the hospital earlier tonight. He was supposed to call me with an update, but he never did. I should go there."

Bobby sits up. "I'll take you."

"Don't be silly."

"Seriously, Taylor: I want to."

She takes a deep breath. "I appreciate the offer, but no. This is a family thing, and no offense, but you'd be a distraction."

Bobby nods. "You're right. I understand."

"Thank you."

"You should call your brother."

"I agree."

Taylor locates her phone and takes it to the bathroom, along with her purse and the rest of her clothes. Seconds later Bobby hears the water running in the sink, same as he heard it the last time she made a call, which means she clearly doesn't want him listening in on her conversations.

He props himself against the pillows in a semi-reclining position and for the first time reads the text Daisy sent earlier about not falling in love with a whore. Then he clicks on the link she sent and learns that Taylor is, in fact, a paid escort. He reads some of her reviews, and frowns.

Is he devastated?

No. But he *is* disappointed.

On the other hand, she never asked him for money, which tells him sure, she's a hooker, but she also has a personal life, and she chose him outside the business, with no expectation of being paid. While it's true he wrote her a check for two thousand dollars, that was *his* idea, not hers, and it was to make up for getting her fired. Is he happy she's an escort? Of course not. But surely she'll stop as soon as they become a couple.

Daisy sends him another text:

Rocco offered Vinny 50 grand to kill you, and Vinny knows you're in Jackson. He doesn't know which hotel, but he'll figure it out soon enough, and he knows some ex-cons there, so you need to leave immediately. Come join me in Memphis. Call and let me know you're on the way. I'm here for you, Bobby. I can help you.

Bobby texts back:

You are so full of shit. You'll be waiting in Memphis? That's a laugh. You didn't even show up for our dinner date. I can't believe anything you say.

Daisy responds:

Is Taylor still with you? Does she know we're texting? What is she doing right now?

Bobby:

Trying to call her brother. Her father's in the hospital.

Daisy:

Don't tell her we're texting. She's bad news.

Bobby:

If she's bad news, what r u? She treated me better than you ever did.

Daisy takes a selfie of her swollen, battered face and sends it with this caption:

Her boyfriend Jeff did this to me. She told him to rob me.

Bobby:

He beat you up and shaved your head? I don't believe you.

Daisy:

I shaved my own head, dumb ass. Taylor's probably trying to call Jeff right now. Be careful.

Bobby:

Sorry about your face. Did Vinny do that?

Daisy:

I told you: Taylor's boyfriend, Jeff, from Percola's. Please come to Memphis, Bobby. I can protect you, but you have to hurry!

Bobby:

Sorry. I need to be here for Taylor. Her father's in the hospital. She needs me.

Daisy:

Big mistake, but it's your choice. Good luck, Bobby. Please delete our texts so Vinny won't know I warned you.

Bobby hears the toilet flush, then hears the faucet turn off, and Taylor emerges from the bathroom in a high state of agitation. She says: "The person trying to call you: is it a woman? Is she a cancer patient?"

"I have no clue. I didn't take the call. What's wrong?"

"I think you're lying, but I don't know why."

Bobby says, "I'm not lying. I don't know any cancer patients."

"How long are you planning to be here?"

"Several days."

"Do you want to see me again?"

"Yes, of course."

"Okay. I'll come back in a few hours."

"Please give my best to your father."

After showing him a look that falls somewhere between confusion and disbelief she says, "I'll do that."

After she leaves, Bobby packs his gear in his backpack, gets in his car, and calls Daisy. When she answers, he says, "I'm on my way."

"Thank God! What changed your mind?"

"I've been to prison."

She pauses. "Say it better. It's late, and my ears are ringing from getting punched in the face."

"In prison, do you know what the preferred method of currency is?"

"Cigarettes?"

"Nope, Ramen noodles. They're worth two dollars in prison currency."

"Why are you telling me this?"

"Because inmates will kill you for a brick of ramen."

"So?"

"You said Vinny knows some ex-cons in Jackson."

"He does. Good point."

Chapter 47

NOW THAT BOBBY'S on his way to Memphis, it's time for Daisy to call the one person in the world she trusts: Sophie Alexander. Bobby needs a fake ID and Sophie's uncle happens to be Sal Bonadello, crime boss for the Midwestern United States, which makes him just as powerful—if not more so—than his Northeast and Southeast counterparts, Vinny and Rocco.

If anyone can get Bobby quick service on a fake ID, it's Sal. But will Sophie do her this huge favor? It helps that Sophie was Daisy's former lover, and the only woman with whom she's been intimate.

Less helpful, Sophie happens to be Dani Ripper's current live-in lover.

Least helpful, prior to meeting Bobby in Louisiana, Daisy stopped in Nashville, seduced Sophie, who—right in the middle of their lovemaking—became consumed by guilt, threw Daisy out of her house, and told her never to contact her, ever again.

So this is a tough call. Yes, Daisy agreed never to tell Dani what transpired between them, and never to call or bother Sophie again for the rest of her life, and that was...

That was three days ago.

She can only imagine how furious Sophie's gonna be to get this call. But Daisy has no choice: Bobby gave her five hundred thousand dollars and his life's in danger. She *has* to make this call.

And Sophie has to come through.

Daisy picks up her phone, notes the time, and shakes her head.

It's really late.

On the bright side, according to Sophie, she and Dani don't sleep in the same bed. If that's true, she might be able to pull this off without causing friction between Sophie and Dani. So she starts with a text:

Sophie, don't freak. I need a simple favor for a close friend. If you were telling the truth about Dani sleeping upstairs, she shouldn't have heard your phone chime just now. I don't want to call, because that could wake her up. So please call me immediately.

Thanks,

Leah

She presses "send" waits a moment, then gets a reply:

Leah: I told you to never call me again. I chose Dani. Deal with it.

Daisy expected worse. But she plods on:

My friend Bobby needs a fake ID tomorrow. His life's in danger. Please, just do me this one favor and I'll never bother you again.

Sophie:

I don't give a shit what happens to your friend Bobby. Or you, for that matter. Dani and I have a good thing going and I won't let you ruin it. I'm serious, Leah: do not call me again, or you'll regret it.

Daisy grits her teeth and curses herself silently. Time to play her trump card. She texts:

It pains me to do this, but I can't let Bobby die. They say a picture is worth a thousand words. If that's true, then surely this video is worth a fake ID.

She attaches the video she made surreptitiously the morning they made love. Daisy recorded it for her eyes only, a sweet remembrance of a special moment that would never be repeated. The first part is voice-only, while her phone was in her hip pocket. The second part is sexual sounds and a video of the ceiling that occurred when she placed her phone on Sophie's bed. The third and final part was hand-held, what a voyeur site would describe as "Unaware Closeup" which means while going down on her former lover, Daisy captured sufficient "selfie" video footage to positively identify the nude woman receiving oral pleasure as Sophie Alexander. And yes, the video clearly shows Sophie was not only a willing participant, but an eager one, fully in the throes of ecstasy. Daisy previously erased the portion of the video where Sophie flipped out seconds later, and started screaming about what a terrible mistake she'd made.

Fifteen minutes later, Sophie responds:

I can't believe you did this to me. That you'd spit on our beautiful history and tape me in a moment of weakness and use it to blackmail me. So this is how it's going to be? Every time you need something you're going to threaten me with this video? Go to hell, Leah. You're dead to me. Yes, you can have your fucking ID. Tell your boyfriend to go to Cincinnati. I'll text you the information when I get it. And fuck you both.

As the tears flow freely down her face, Daisy texts:

I'm so very sorry, Sophie. I know you won't believe this, but it was never my intention to use this video against you. But without a new ID, Bobby will be dead within days. So thank you. But please don't live in fear. I promise not to ever threaten you again. My heart is aching. I will always love you, and will always treasure our history.

She doesn't expect a response from Sophie, and nor does she get one.

Chapter 48

THE KNOCK AT her door wakes her up. Sleepily, Daisy turns on a lamp, climbs out of bed, lets Bobby in and gives him a big hug.

"Thanks for coming," she says, holding a hand in front of her face. "You need to pee or something?"

"I do." He sets his backpack on the floor, fishes his Dopp kit from it, and carries it into the bathroom. After peeing, washing his face and brushing his teeth, he exits to see her sitting on the side of the bed in relative darkness, illuminated only by the bathroom light behind him.

He says, "Can you turn the lamp back on?"

"I'd rather not."

He makes his way to the bed and when he sits beside her she says, "I owe you an apology."

"Just one?"

"Several."

"I agree."

"I'm sorry, Bobby."

"It's okay. I still love you."

She laughs. "How's that possible?"

He shrugs. "You're here, I'm here."

"I stood you up."

"Yeah, but you also went to the trouble of trying to find a replacement."

"Did you like her?"

"Yeah. Sort of. I mean, she's not *you*. She's upbeat. Perky. Sweet."

"I can be sweet."

"You can?"

She laughs.

Bobby says, "Not only did you find a replacement, you also got me laid. At least, I *think* you did."

Daisy says nothing.

"Did you pay Taylor to fuck me?"

She nods in the dark, but he probably can't see, so she confirms it verbally, "Yes. Are you pissed?"

"*Pissed?* Hell *no!* It was the best—" He pauses. "I mean, no. I'm not pissed."

"The best what?"

"Huh?"

"You said it was the best, and I asked, 'best what?'"

"What do you mean?"

"Were you actually going to sit there and tell me Taylor gave you the best sex of your life?"

"No, of course not."

"Then what did you mean?"

"It was the best gesture you could have made."

She laughs. "Liar!"

"I would never lie to you!"

"Never? Glad to hear it! That means I can ask you a direct question and get an honest answer. So here goes: was Taylor the best sex you ever had?"

He sighs. "Yes."

"That's wonderful!"

"It is?"

"Of course. It means the beating I took wasn't a complete disaster. It means my money wasn't wasted. And it means we can get some sleep tonight without any sexual pressure."

"What do you mean?"

"I'm tired and beat up and my head hurts like crazy. But if you hadn't gotten laid, not to mention the best sex of your entire *life*, I'd feel obligated to put out for you."

"You would?"

"Of course."

"Why?"

"I owe you."

"Is that the only reason?"

"No. Also, I find you attractive. Did you guys use a condom?"

"We did, actually."

"Where'd you get it?"

"She had one."

"She probably buys them in bulk, directly from the warehouse. Probably backs her car up to the loading dock and has the forklift driver slide a whole pallet of them right into her trunk."

Considering this a perfect time to change the subject, Bobby says, "Can I turn the lamp back on?"

"Why?"

"I'd like to see your face. It looked awful in the pic you sent."

"I'd rather you didn't."

"Like I said, I already saw the picture."

"It's worse now. Much more swollen."

"Can I at least give you one of my pain pills?"

"No. But thanks."

Bobby says, "There's something I couldn't help but notice the moment I entered the room."

"What's that?"

"There's only one bed."

"It's a king. There's plenty of room for both of us. What's the problem?"

"Music to my ears!" he says, kicking off his shoes. He removes his socks and starts unbuttoning his shirt.

"Don't get any ideas," she says.

He rolls his eyes in the dark and continues disrobing. Now, standing tall in his underwear, she says, "Get naked."

"Really?"

"Yes. Then march your ass into the bathroom and take a hot, soapy shower and stay in there till you've removed every last fume of whore scent from your body."

He laughs, then does as he's told. And returns ten minutes later to find her sleeping. He circles the bed, climbs in, and nestles up against her.

"You awake?" he whispers.

"Mmmf. No."

A minute passes. Then she says, "What are you *doing?*"

"Nothing!"

"Why not?"

"What do you mean?"

"We're in bed, I'm completely naked, and—"

"You're *naked?*"

"You couldn't tell?"

"No. I mean, it's dark. You're under the covers."

"You didn't peek when I was asleep just now?"

"Of *course* not!"

"Why not?"

"You said not to get any ideas."

She laughs. "Well, what did you *expect* me to say? I'm not a whore, like all your other girlfriends."

"One whore. Supplied by you. And you specifically said, 'Don't get any ideas.'"

"That's because ideas aren't your strong point," she says, laughing.

"You are such a smart ass!"

"Thank you. I used to be a dumb ass, but everyone kept calling me Bobby."

"Ouch."

If he didn't know better he'd swear she's trying to engage in pre-sexual banter. But this would be their what, third attempt? And the other two were interrupted at the last second by ants and mobsters. And what if she's just teasing him? Yes, she naked, but she's also half-asleep, not facing him, and in a lot of pain. He needs her to give him one more sign before he's convinced she's finally going to give it up.

And then she does: "I'm still naked," she purrs.

"Me too."

"Say something sweet."

"Like what?"

"Tell me what's on your mind right now."

"I never did it with a bald girl before."

She sighs. "That's your best effort?"

"No. But it's what I was thinking just then."

She pauses. "You know I'm not bald, right?"

"I know."

Just as he thinks he blew it she says, "Have you always *wanted* to do it with a bald girl?"

"Not till tonight."

"*Bobby!*"

"What?"

"That was actually sort of romantic!"

He scoots over till their bodies are touching. Then places his hand on her thigh, and works it up to her... "Hey! You're not naked!"

Daisy giggles. "Not yet. But if you ask me nicely to remove my clothes..."

"Would you please remove your clothes?"

"No. But *you* can, if you'd like."

Chapter 49

"WELL?" BOBBY SAYS, imperiously.

What the *fuck*? Did he just slap her *ass*?

Daisy frowns, squints against the sunlight peeking through the curtain space.

"Well?" he repeats.

"Well, what?" she says, in a mood.

"How was it?"

Omigod! Did he actually, no shit, just ask her that?

He did.

She yawns, props up on one elbow, and turns to face him.

"Are you *smirking*?"

"Probably."

"Jesus, Robert. Act like you've been there before."

"Say whatever you want. You can't hurt my feelings. Not today."

"Why not?"

"Because we finally did it. And you were great." When she fails to respond, a look of concern crosses his face. "Did I hurt you?"

"Don't flatter yourself."

"No, I meant—"

He focuses on her face. The angry bruise beside her mouth is at least three shades of black. Her cheek has swollen to half-again its normal size, and the eye above it is blood red. Jeff the waiter's a big guy. She's lucky as hell her nose wasn't broken during the attack, not to mention her jaw. As Bobby instinctively reaches toward her face, Daisy recoils.

"Don't touch me!" she says, and flips back to her original position on the bed and closes her eyes.

"*Jesus*, Daisy. I wasn't gonna *hurt* you!"

She says nothing.

Bobby slides off the bed, walks to the bathroom. After peeing, he brushes his teeth, washes his hands, locates a pain pill, and brings it to her.

"Here," he says. "Take this. You'll feel a lot better."

"No thanks," she says, with zero appreciation behind her words. Bobby lashes out: "Why are you being so *mean* to me? Are you having second thoughts?"

She grits her teeth. "You *really* want to know?"

"Please."

"I don't like being slapped awake. Especially after being up most of the night with a horrible headache and pains from bruises where I wasn't even punched. Are you aware I took a ten-minute shower in the middle of the night and washed and dried my hair?"

"You *did? Why?*"

"Because I threw up, Bobby. I think I've got a concussion."

"We should get you to a doctor."

"Ya think?"

He sighs. "I'm sorry about the smirk. I thought things went really well last night, and I was super excited and hoped you felt the same way. The slap was a bad idea, though it was meant to be more like a love pat. But it was thoughtless of me to forget about your pain. I know you're upset, but I wish you'd take this pill. I know from personal experience it'll make you feel a lot better. And if you're worried about driving, I'll do whatever driving that needs to be done."

"Thank you, Bobby. As far as apologies go, that was a good one. Just so you know, your slap wasn't the only thing that pissed me off."

"What else did I do?"

"I couldn't believe you expected me to give you a sexual critique hours after crowing that Taylor gave you the best sex of your life."

"I...I wasn't *comparing*, or anything, I just—"

"It's okay. I wasn't expecting to outfuck a whore. I'm just explaining my mood, so you won't think I'm this bitchy every morning."

"You couldn't be!"

She smiles despite her annoyance. "Anyway, I can't take the pill."

"Why not?"

"I already stole one from you while you were sleeping. What time is it?"

"About eight-fifteen."

She bolts upright. "Shit! We need to get moving."

"What's the rush?"

"Our flight leaves at 10:33."

"Our *what?*"

"I booked us a flight to Cincinnati. Your new identity, remember?"

"Why Cincinnati?"

"That's where my contact is. Why are you looking at me like that? You think I'm *lying?* You think I'm setting you *up?*"

"Not if you *say* you aren't."

"I'm not. You're getting a new ID. That's all."

"Then what?"

"Then, whatever you want. Dinner? Drinks?"

"Sex?"

"It's possible. I already booked a hotel room in case the ID takes longer than expected."

"How long should it take?"

"No way of knowing."

"What time's the appointment?"

"We don't have one yet. Hence, the hotel."

He laughs. "Hence?"

She turns on the TV and says, "Holy Shit!"

A local news anchor is showing footage of an explosion that took place the previous night in a Memphis suburb. According to the voice-over, a SWAT team rescued a woman named Vicki Armstrong from a local home where she'd been held captive by a serial killer. Daisy follows the story for a couple of minutes, then says, "Are you done in the bathroom?"

"Yes."

"Then stand aside and let me work my magic. In the meantime, keep watching and let me know if they explain why that woman's holding her hands up like she's signaling a touchdown."

Chapter 50

WHEN THEIR PLANE touches down in Cincinnati, Daisy switches her phone off Airport Mode and finds a text message from Sophie that contains three items: a time, an address, and a contact person. She turns to Bobby. "We're on!"

"What time?"

"Three-fifteen."

"That gives us more than two hours. You want to get some lunch or try for an early check-in at the hotel?"

"Lunch. I'm starving."

"Me too!"

They search the Internet for restaurants near the Mothers of Sicily Charity Center, where they're supposed to show up at 3:15 p.m. and ask for a guy named Ralphie. After settling on a place that describes itself as "an authentic rustic Italian eatery", they fetch their bags from baggage claim and hail a cab. Forty minutes later they're munching on breadsticks, waiting on pasta. At 3:15, in the Mother's of Sicily foyer, they ask for Ralphie, and two large men—old, with disfigured faces— show up and escort them down a long hall that leads to an ancient staircase, which they descend. They're ushered into a throwback office decorated in 70's Naugahyde, green and gold. They're asked to take a seat, and they do. Then they gasp simultaneously as they receive identical injections at the base of their necks. When Daisy wakes up, she's all alone in a room composed entirely of concrete, except for a steel door. Inside the room are four items: a bed, a sink, a toilet, and a wall-mounted camera, all of which confirms what she suspected the moment she opened her eyes: she's being held prisoner.

Should she shout?

She can think of a dozen reasons not to, and only one why she should:

Bobby.

Is he in a similar room? Could he be in an adjoining cell?

She calls his name, then listens. Then calls it again, louder.

Then she screams it, but receives no response.

An hour passes, or possibly two, before she hears footsteps approaching. Moments later, the door opens, and a man enters.

"How do you feel?" he asks.

"Shitty. Where's Bobby?"

"How about I tell you what I know, and when I'm done you can tell me what you'd *like* to know. Will that work?"

She nods.

He says, "You have an old phone. Only four numbers in the password. You know how many combinations that makes?"

"Ten thousand."

He looks at her with a combination of surprise and genuine respect. Then says, "We've got someone working on it, but if you want to make her job easier, you can tell me the combination and I'll relay it to her."

"Seven-seven-five-one."

"Thank you."

He looks at the camera and nods. Then says, "Have you heard of Sal Bonadello?"

"Yes."

"I'm his associate. The reason you and I are having this chat is because you threatened his niece, Sophie Alexander. By the way, I'm Ralphie."

"Hello. I'm Daisy."

"According to the various passports in your belongings, you're several people. Is Daisy Pepper your preference?"

"Yes."

"Very well. So, Daisy: it's imperative you understand what I'm about to say. There are consequences for threatening Mr. Bonadello's family members. If you had any type of experience with our business you'd already be dead. But you're a civilian, so we're gonna explain how things work, and give you a second chance. But only one, understand?"

"Yes, sir. Thank you."

"Unfortunately, second chances don't come cheap. We typically charge an arm."

"Excuse me?"

"We usually give you a warning, and cut off an arm. But in your case, we're not gonna do that. Do you know why?"

"Because Sophie's my friend?"

"Former friend. Lucky for you, she asked Mr. Bonadello to spare your arm, and he agreed."

"Please let her know I'm grateful."

"She and I don't speak."

Not knowing how to respond, Daisy says nothing, which prompts Ralphie to say: "The good news is you get to keep your arm. The bad news is you have to remain in this cell."

"How long?"

"I asked Mr. Bonadello the same question, and he said, 'Until her hair grows six inches.'"

"*What?*"

"Six inches."

Daisy instinctively runs her hand over her scalp, but Ralphie says, "Not *that* hair," and Daisy's eyes go wide. Not because it proves Sal Bonadello has seen her naked and apparently intends to *continue* seeing her naked—or at least not *just* because of that. But because she happens to know that pubic hair is genetically predisposed to grow to a maximum length that rarely exceeds one-and-a-half inches. Which means she could be locked in this room for the rest of her life.

Lightheaded, close to fainting, Daisy lurches forward, head down, to keep from passing out.

In the nick of time, a loud voice booms through the speaker: "Quit fuckin' with her, Ralphie!"

"I was just kiddin'," Ralphie says. "It's the hair on your head. When it grows six inches, you're done."

She looks up. "You swear?"

He nods.

She looks around the room till she locates the speaker from which the voice emanated. She didn't notice earlier, but it's built into the base of the camera. "You're seriously planning to hold me prisoner for a year?"

"A year?"

"Head hair grows a half-inch per month. That's six inches a year."

"How do you *know* that?"

"I have some medical training."

"So do I, but I didn't know *that*! Jeez. Seems like a long time for just six inches of hair."

"I agree."

"Then again, it beats losin' an arm."

"Where's Bobby? Did they let him go?"

"I don't know."

"Bobby had nothing to do with this! He doesn't even have a clue who Sophie *is*! He just needs an ID."

Ralphie shrugs. "I ain't the boss."

She looks up at the camera. "Please: let Bobby go. He's completely innocent in this."

The voice on the speaker says, "You had four phones, three ID's, and more than thirty grand in your suitcase. What's that all about?"

Daisy sighs. "Whoever you are, can you please show yourself? I'll tell you everything you want to know, but only if you give Bobby a new ID and let him go."

The voice says, "Sorry," and nothing more.

Daisy looks at Ralphie and whispers, "Can you find out for me?"

He whispers back, "I can try."

"Thank you."

Chapter 51

AUTHORS'NOTE: SURE, I could devote an entire chapter explaining how worried, lonely, and miserable Daisy was over the first six months of her captivity, and I could really ramp up the prose and bore you to tears ala Melville's Chapter 42 of *Moby Dick*, titled "The Whiteness of the Whale," wherein 3,645 words are used to explain how white Moby Dick was. While I hate to miss out on the opportunity to publish a book The New York Times might consider "an instant classic," it would be a complete and utter waste of your time to have to read it.

So, trust me when I tell you that absolutely nothing of consequence happened during the first six months of Daisy's captivity that you could possibly care about, other than her realization she's pregnant with Bobby's child.

Chapter 52

ONCE A MONTH throughout her captivity, Sal Bonadello's personal physician came to visit her, and each time he did, her life improved. He's the one responsible for getting her the privacy curtain, the feminine products, the pre-natal vitamins, the daily walks, the balanced diet, and the cable TV. After the doctor's sixth visit, Ralphie informed her she'd be released after serving only three inches of her six-inch sentence.

As instant tears puddled in her eyes, Daisy said, "They're letting me *go?* Swear to God?"

"Yup."

"*When?*"

"Today. But first, you gotta hear the lecture."

The lecture started with a series of graphic, detailed threats and ended with news related to Bobby Cujo. The threats delineated everything that would happen to her should she attempt to contact Sophie Alexander, or any of Sophie's friends, relatives, or associates, ever again.

The news about Bobby was the first she'd received since her initial confinement, despite the fact she begged him every day to tell her if Bobby was okay.

As it turns out, he was.

With one notable exception.

Chapter 53

"ON THE ONE hand," Ralphie said, "Bobby's alive. On the other... well, he ain't *got* another."

"Another what?"

"Hand."

"*What?*"

"Remember how I told you the civilian penalty for fuckin' with family members is you lose an arm? Well, Bobby lost an arm."

Daisy burst into tears. So distraught was she, it took Ralphie more than fifteen minutes to calm her down. When he finally managed it, she whimpered and lamented, "It's all my fault."

Ralphie said, "You're right. It is."

"Where is he?"

"Long gone."

"What do you mean?"

"We took care of him. Gave him a fake ID, moved him to a new town."

"Where?"

"Can't tell you."

"Why not? I need to *see* him!"

"Sorry."

"I'm carrying his *baby*!"

"You don't know that for sure."

Ralphie was right. She could have been carrying Vinny's baby. And if she was, God help her if the baby winds up inheriting her and Vinny's worst traits.

"Why won't you tell me where Bobby is?"

"I got orders."

"Will you at least tell me his new name?"

"Nope."

"Why not?"

"He's workin' for *us*, now."

"What does *that* mean?"

"It means he started a new life, and he blames you for losing his arm, and he never wants to see or hear from you ever again."

"I don't believe that."

Ralphie shrugged.

She said, "I need to hear *him* tell me that, face to face."

"You *need* that, do you? Well, I need to be 20 years old again, only this time a rock star. You know what you and I should do?"

"What's that?"

"Talk to my mom."

"Why?"

"Because the whole time I was growin' up she said: 'Tell me what you *need*, and I'll tell you how to live without it.'"

Epilogue

SAL BONADELLO KEPT all but a thousand dollars of the money Daisy had in her suitcases, but was nice enough to return her phones and ID's, which allowed her to finally meet with Lucy Lincoln, the Nashville banker, who, for a fee, offered to help Daisy move her money overseas. Daisy listened to Lucy's pitch, but had already decided not to expatriate. She told Lucy she was going to keep her checking account in Nashville for the time being. After presenting her Daisy Pepper ID, she withdrew $9,000 from her account and promptly moved to Charleston, South Carolina, a town she had fallen in love with while getting hooked on the reality TV show, *Southern Charm*.

From that day forward, Daisy began using the new name and ID she purchased in Bangkok when Jake Cujo stood her up. Unlike her other fake names, Daisy selected this one with great care. She wanted a name that was so common even nosey people would find it difficult, if not impossible, to run a successful background check on her. So she decided to assume the tenth most common female's name in North America, and the tenth most common surname. Which is how she became...Samantha Wilson.

As far as the bank in Nashville could tell, Daisy Pepper moved to Charleston, South Carolina, made a hefty down payment on a three-bedroom condo, and hired a personal live-in assistant named Samantha Wilson, to whom she paid a weekly salary of $1,500. The bank had no reason to know or care that three months later Samantha Wilson gave birth to a daughter named Aria, which happened to be the tenth most common baby girl's name in North America that year.

Not that the bank in Nashville would know or care, but a few months after giving birth, Samantha scored a second job bartending on weekends at a local nightspot. A year later, after "negotiating" the real estate deal of the century (she legally purchased Daisy Pepper's condo for nothing more than the amount of the existing mortgage) Samantha's identity, job history, and residence were permanently established.

In the weeks and months before Aria was born...

Daisy spent hours searching the Internet for news about Bobby, Jake, and even Eileen. But the only thing she could determine for certain was all three were missing. She tracked down the phone number for Bobby's trailer park booty-call girlfriend, Stacy, and purchased a new burner phone for the single purpose of calling her, but Stacy had nothing to offer. Daisy even called Sallee Hospital and asked Horace Boudreaux, Executive Director of Operations, if Bobby ever showed up to claim the settlement money. He had not, so Daisy told him to wire her portion of the settlement to her account in Nashville, and he did.

Daisy widened her search to include news about one-armed men, and new religious shrines, and Moon Pies that resembled John the Baptist, but nothing of substance ever turned up. If Ralphie was right about Bobby working for Sal Bonadello, he would almost certainly have to be living in the Midwestern United States, which was Sal's territory, so she placed a greater emphasis on targeting those states.

Unfortunately, it's a vast area that includes more than a hundred million residents.

Her last-ditch effort may have been her best: she called the Cane River Bank & Trust, the bank Bobby used to wire her the half-million. She told the manager she'd been cleaning out her dresser drawer and discovered an uncashed check from her old friend, Bobby Cujo, in the amount of $300. Knowing it was seven months old, she wanted to know if there were sufficient funds in his account to cover it. The manager informed her she'd have to contact Mr. Cujo directly, since he was no longer a customer of the bank.

And so, with Aria's birth imminent, after registering all the names and categories with the various Internet search engines, Daisy decided to move forward with her life. In an ideal world, she would have found Bobby, they would have gotten married and raised the baby together. But she was no closer to finding him and had no evidence he was even searching for her. Could it be true Ralphie was being honest? That Bobby wanted nothing to do with her? True or not, Aria needed her time more than Bobby, and so she limited her search to checking her email box whenever Yahoo, or Bing, or Google Search, got a hit. But nothing of substance ever showed up.

Until it did.

The hit came from a Google Search of the words "Moon Pie Shrine." Upon opening the link, her excitement quickly faded as she realized it was a different version of the same press release she had received twice before from the Bell Buckle Tennessee Chamber of Commerce announcing their annual RC-Moon Pie Festival, which takes place on the third Saturday in June, and claims to attract visitors from all over the world.

Only this time Daisy decided to go and to take Aria with her.

On the afternoon of the first day, while sitting at a picnic table in Bell Buckle, Tennessee, as Aria was nibbling on her free Moon Pie, Daisy heard snippets of a conversation from a nearby table: a man was saying, "People came from all over the world to see it," and the other people at the table laughed. Daisy laughed, too, as it reminded her of Bobby and his True Believers. But when the man said, "It looked exactly like John the Baptist!" her heart leaped.

She told Aria to stay put, then made a wide circle around the table to get a better look at the man from a distance.

And there was no mistake: it was Bobby.

But even though he was boisterously regaling the table with conversation, he looked up, and when their eyes met, he dropped his RC Cola on the table, and everyone around him jumped to avoid the splash.

And that's when Daisy saw the ring on his finger, and the women at his side. She rushed back to her table, scooped Aria up in her arms, and tried to get away. But Bobby caught up to them and said, "Jesus, Daisy! Is it really *you?*"

"Hey, Bobby."

"They told me you were dead."

"They told me they cut your arm off, and that you never wanted to see me again."

Confused, he looked down at the little girl. "Who's this?"

"My daughter, Aria."

Bobby looked around. "Where's the father?" Then it hit him, and his eyes went wide. He dropped to a knee to get a better look, but being shy, Aria moved behind Daisy's legs. Then the wife showed up, saying, "Steve? Is everything alright?"

Daisy said, "Hi Abby."

The former Abby Dale, from ItsJustCoffee.co cocked her head. "Have we met?"

"Once, a long time ago. Congratulations on your marriage."

It took Abby several seconds, then it registered. She looked at Aria, then cast an accusing look at Bobby, and said, "How long have you known about this?"

"Fifteen seconds."

"Right. And she just happened to show up in the same hick town at the same time with your *daughter*? Bullshit! You said she was dead."

"I thought she was. And yes, it's a coincidence, and no, I had no idea there was a child." To Daisy, Bobby said, "We need to sit down and talk about this."

"There's nothing to talk about, *Steve*. This is Vinny's daughter."

"*What*? That's crazy! *Look* at her!"

"I have. Every single day for the past two-and-a-half years."

Bobby did the math in his head. "She's got to be at least three. How old are you, Aria?"

Aria said nothing.

Daisy said, "This is Vinny's child. If you'd ever met him, you'd see the resemblance."

Bobby wasn't buying it. "What name are you using these days?"

"Daisy Pepper."

Aria laughed out loud.

Bobby said, "I know better. I searched for you for months." To Aria, he said: "What's your mom's name?"

Aria looked at her mom but said nothing.

"Where do you live?"

Aria said, "Mommy? I'm scared."

Daisy said, "It was nice to see you again, but we need to go."

"Where are you staying?"

"Holiday Inn."

"You swear?"

She nodded.

Bobby's face was filled with concern. "Please, Daisy. For once in your life, do the right thing. Don't deny me the chance to be involved in Aria's life."

Daisy gave him a long look that ended with a deep sigh. "I wish she *was* your daughter. As you know, Vinny isn't the world's greatest role model. But still, I'd love to know what happened to you, and Jake, and Eileen. Is there any way we could all get together this afternoon and catch up on what's happened in our lives?"

Abby spoke up: "I'd say no, since one of us needs to be the voice of reason. None of us are who we were, and nothing good can come from sharing that information." She paused. "Unless you're willing to go on record about the paternity issue."

Daisy wondered what happened to the woman Bobby once described as *upbeat, perky, and sweet.* "How about this," she said. "Come to our hotel this afternoon, Room 217. Or follow us there now, if you like. And whenever you get there, I'll furnish proof she's Vinny's daughter."

"What proof could you possibly have?"

"Her passport."

Abby looked confused.

Daisy said, "It shows her date of birth."

Without even looking at Bobby, Abby said, "We'll be there in an hour. And I *would* like to photograph any documentation you have, and get your further reassurance that in the years to come, regardless of your lifestyle choices, Steve and I won't be expected to provide support for a child that isn't his."

"I'll be happy to put all that in writing before you arrive," Daisy said.

"We'd like that," Abby said.

Of course, Daisy and Aria weren't staying at the Holiday Inn. And there was no passport. And Vinny wasn't the father. And there was no way Daisy was going to let Abby and Bobby—or Steve, as he's now called—within an inch of her daughter. Not because she doesn't care for Bobby, and not because he wouldn't be a wonderful dad, but because he knows far too much about her past, and because Jordan—the owner of the hotspot where she works on weekends, who also happens to be her fiancé—would likely bolt if she were to introduce another element into their relationship. For these reasons and others, Daisy steered her car through the streets of Bell Buckle, then merged onto the highway, increased her speed, and never looked back.

The End

Author's Note:

BE SURE TO check out the companion novel to *Daisy & Bobby*. It's titled *Hot Mess Express*, and I think you'll find it a fun romp that intersects with some of the characters, settings, and situations you encountered in this book.

As you must know by now, I love writing novels! But what I love even more is hearing from readers. If you enjoyed this or any of my other books it would mean the world to me if you'd click the link below so you can be on my notification list. That way you can receive updates, contests, prizes, and savings of up to 67% on eBooks immediately after publication!

Just click this link: http://www.DonovanCreed.com, and I'll personally thank you for trying my books.

Also, if you get a chance, I hope you'll check out Dani Ripper's website:

http://www.daniripper.com

Personal Message from John Locke:

I love writing books! But what I love even more is hearing from readers. If you enjoyed this or any of my other books it would mean the world to me if you'd click the link below so you can be on my notification list. That way you can receive updates, contests, prizes, and savings of up to 67% on eBooks immediately after publication!

Just access this link: http://www.DonovanCreed.com, and I'll personally thank you for trying my books.

Also, if you get a chance, I hope you'll check out Dani's website:

http://www.daniripper.com

John Locke

New York Times Best Selling Author

Guinness World Record Holder for eBook Sales!

Fastest Author in History to sell 1 million eBooks!

8th Member of the Kindle Million Sales Club

(Members include James Patterson, George R.R. Martin, and Lee Child)

John Locke had 4 of the top 10 eBooks on

Amazon/Kindle at the same time, including #1 and #2!

...Had 6 of the top 20 books at the same time!

...Had 8 books in the top 43 at the same time!

...Has written 33 books in five years in six separate genres,

All best-sellers!

...Has been published throughout the world in numerous languages

by the world's most prestigious publishing houses!

...Winner, Second Act Magazine's Story of the Year!

...Named by Time Magazine as one of the "Stars of the DIY-Publishing Era"

Wall Street Journal: "John Locke (is) transforming the 'book' business"

Donovan Creed Series:

Lethal People
Lethal Experiment
Saving Rachel
Now & Then
Wish List
A Girl Like You
Vegas Moon
The Love You Crave
Maybe
Callie's Last Dance
Because We Can!
This Means War!

Emmett Love Series:

Follow the Stone
Don't Poke the Bear
Emmett & Gentry
Goodbye, Enorma
Rag Soup
Spider Rain

Dani Ripper Series:

Call Me!
Promise You Won't Tell?
Teacher, Teacher
Don't Tell Presley!
Abbey Rayne
Hot Mess Express

Dr. Gideon Box Series:

Bad Doctor
Box
Outside the Box
Boxed In!

Other:

Kill Jill
Casting Call
When David Died
Sorority Girl
Daisy & Bobby

Kindle Worlds:

A Kiss for Luck (Kindle Only)

Non-Fiction:

How I sold 1 Million eBooks in 5 Months!

Made in the USA
Middletown, DE
25 July 2020

13129217R00133